ORDER OF THE SEERS

THE LAST SEER

CERECE RENNIE MURPHY

Published by LionSky Publishing

Cover design by Kea Taylor for Imagine Photography

Interior design by Jessica Tilles for TWA Solutions

Printed in the United States of America

ISBN 13: 978-0-9856210-4-9

Library of Congress Control Number: 2014916239

Dedication

This book is dedicated to you. Yes, YOU—the one
holding this book. Through the span of more than three
years and three books, you have trusted me, waited for
me, and allowed me to share this story with you. From
the first person to ever read *Order of the Seers*, to those of
you who I will never meet, know that you have touched
me, inspired and humbled me.

I hope, in some way, this story has done
the same for you.

May you take hold of your light and shine it
for all of us to see.

Best Always,
Cerece

Other Titles by Cerece Rennie Murphy

Order of the Seers — *Book I*

Order of the Seers: The Red Order — *Book II*

Order of the Seers: The Last Seer — *Book III*

Acknowledgements

Usually, this section is easy to do, but I guess because it's the last book in the Trilogy I want to make SURE I get it right. There are so many people to thank for helping me and encouraging me on this journey.

First and foremost, to my husband, Sekou Murphy. Three years ago, I told you that I wanted to quit my job so that I could finish writing this story that I had in my head. With no plan to publish or figure out IF it could make any money, you told me, "Go ahead. We'll figure it out." Thank you for being my partner, my biggest fan and my husband. I love you.

To my Mom, Jemma Baptiste Rennie, you have believed in me since before I took my first breath. You are the source of every good thing in my life. Thank you for teaching me what it means to love another human being with your whole heart.

To my big sister, Monica, my big brother Al and my best friend, Kamishia, thank you for seeing me truly and loving me anyway. Your love gives me courage to try, while never taking myself too seriously.

To my editors, Jessica Faulkner, Stephanie Carnes and Quiana Goodrum. Thank you for blessing me with your talents, insight and knowledge. Not only is *Order of the Seers* a better story because of your contributions, but you also made me look good, even though I *still* don't know where that comma goes!

To Trice Hickman, Ella Curry, Kea Taylor, Jessica Tilles, Lynn "Gangsta in Pearls" Emery, Annette Stone, and my RIB family, thank you for giving me your friendship and your expertise so freely. Each of you has coached me through the maze of becoming an author. It still scares me, but I know so much more now and it shows.

To Kenya McGuire Johnson and Bettina Lanyi, fellow travelers on the path of "Continually Putting Yourself Out There". Thank you for listening to my doubts and fears, then telling me "You can do it, Cerece. Keep going." Kindred spirits are hard to find. So glad I have you both.

To Robert L. Moore, I will never forget what you taught me. I'm beginning to believe. To Seth Godin, for still coaching people you've never met. You're a gift from God, whether you know it or not.

And to the readers, thank you for picking up my books and giving them a chance to settle in and take hold. Each of you is a dream come true.

For our struggle is not against flesh and blood, but against the rulers, against the authorities, against the powers of this dark world and against the spiritual forces of evil in the heavenly realms.

– Ephesians 6:12

ORDER OF THE SEERS

THE LAST SEER

PROLOGUE

The Cover of Darkness

Bamiyan Province, Afghanistan

The high-pitched wail of the creatures was deafening as their black wings beat against the red sky. From the caves scraped out of the mountainside, the valley looked desolate, a place of ruin. Beasts ruled the heavens as the damned lay broken below. And in between, Ghazal, and what was left of her village, huddled, trapped between two hells.

Whether anyone else in the world was aware of what was happening to them, Ghazal had no way of knowing. With the preparations for her dowry, her family didn't have the money to replace their old TV when it died and the radio they had was gone—smashed to pieces in the rush to escape the creatures that now held them confined in their cave.

Barely half an hour before, while the watchmen were catching their first glimpse of something on the horizon, Ghazal's neighbors had only just entered her home, carrying news of strange sightings from around the world—Geneva, London, Paris—places she had read about, but was sure she would never see.

Though at first their forms were little more than blotches against the setting sun, the screeching sounds that echoed before them erased any doubt in the watchmen's minds about the nature of what approached. Whatever it was meant them harm. They sounded the alarm. Her betrothed, her father, and all the other men of the valley ran forth to set a perimeter and face the threat head on.

The clerics, the women, and the children were left behind to run and endure as best they could.

It was just as in her vision.

At the time, Ghazal had called after the men wildly, telling them it was useless, but no one listened. She had to be dragged away in her grief as she saw her vision unfold—bodies thrown, fires burning, and the sound of bones crushed under the weight of merciless feet.

Clarity came at the mouth of the precipice. She looked back at those who had carried and comforted her up the mountain one last time before stepping out onto the cliff's edge. The light blue fabric of her burka billowed and soared in the hot air as she leapt off into the unsuspecting clutches of a beast that had no hope of surviving what she could do.

CHAPTER 1: SET IN MOTION

They drove back to Geneva in silence, each consumed by the dread of what was to come. Occasionally, you could hear the soft vibration of Joel's thumb tapping his phone screen as he made arrangements for a plane to take them back to London, but otherwise, no one made a sound. Though unspoken, each of them understood that they were listening for the screeching sounds that had been echoing in their ears ever since they left Crane's castle.

"I'm sorry," Lilli finally said to no one in particular as she stared out of the backseat window. Joel tried to bring her closer into his one-armed embrace, but she resisted, feeling unworthy of the comfort.

"You did everything you could, Lilli. Everything," Joel whispered.

"Yeah. Maybe I did too much. Look at what's happened. There are more, you know, so many more. 'Legions', he said, and I can feel them. I know Maura can too, like a darkness spreading."

"This wasn't your fault," Joel tried again, but his words made no difference.

"He was their leader. He kept them…contained," Lilli continued. "But now…I've unleashed them. They follow no one."

"How do you know this?" Joel asked. He had no choice but to focus on her words. Her mind was moving too fast for him to comprehend.

Lilli turned from the window to face him. For an instant, she wondered why he didn't know the answer, just as she did. But then she felt it, the incongruence in their thoughts. For the first time since they'd met, she realized that her consciousness had become somehow separate from his, and the new distance hurt her deeply.

"Because I *know*." Lilli answered with tears burning in her eyes.

As Joel watched them run silently down her cheeks, he understood what she was trying to tell him. From the place she now inhabited, she could sense them clearly. She could see and understand more than she ever had before.

It won't be long, he thought. *I will join you whenever we decide.*

Lilli nodded her head slightly after shooting a quick glance at Liam in the driver's seat. Closing her eyes, Lilli willed her thoughts to slow until she could feel her connection with Joel restored.

Yes, she answered in relief, *after we tell him. We'll wait until then.*

Having resolved at least one of the many problems that plagued her mind, Lilli finally allowed herself the comfort of Joel's embrace. She'd just begun to release the tension in her body when Liam spoke up.

From the driver's seat, Liam had been listening in on their conversation, hoping to glean something that would explain what they'd witnessed. But just as she and Joel had finally gotten to the heart of his questions, they fell silent. As the quiet stretched on, Liam risked an impatient glance in the rear view mirror to find them engrossed in silent conversation.

"Ah, you guys mind sharing with the rest of the class?" Liam asked. "Who or what was that back there? I'd like to know what we're dealing with."

"The demon you saw was Crane," Lilli explained. "I killed him, but in doing that I think I've unleashed something worse. Something that was at least partially under control before, but now...now, they are more dangerous."

"The creatures..." Liam offered.

"Yes, they were with Crane. But those were just a few. There are more—many more—that have been unleashed because of me."

Liam squinted at his sister in the rearview mirror. "Why do you keep saying that—'because of me'? Even you have blind spots, Lilli. How could you have known? You were fighting for your life." When she didn't immediately disregard what he'd said, Liam seized the chance to ask one of the questions he really wanted to know.

"And how did you kill him, by the way? You didn't even lift a finger. You just...spoke to him. I've never seen you do that before. When did you learn that?"

As Liam was talking, Alessandra turned in her seat to look back at Lilli. She had seen the difference in Lilli as soon as they broke down the castle door. In the heat of the moment, Alessandra hadn't given it any thought, but looking at her now, even the feeling of Lilli's presence in the Collective was different. Brighter, but somehow more dispersed.

Don't say anything! Please! Not yet.

Alessandra heard Lilli's pleading words in her mind clearer than she ever had before. Not spoken through the Collective, but directly into her thoughts.

Why? She asked silently.

Because I am becoming something different…

Alessandra eyed Lilli and Joel suspiciously, but said nothing as she processed the warning in Lilli's words—the clear notion that "different" was not a good thing in this case. *Liam*, she realized. *This is about protecting Liam.*

Yes, Lilli answered while keeping her outward attention on her brother.

Alessandra hesitated for only a moment before turning back around in her seat. Whatever Lilli had to say would hurt Liam and as far as Alessandra was concerned, there was no need to do that now.

Before her silent exchange with Alessandra was over, Lilli answered her brother aloud, as if theirs was the only conversation taking place.

"No, I didn't know this would happen, but I should have tried to see it. I was just so focused on him not hurting me or you guys that I just wanted him gone."

Liam was quiet again, considering the few facts he knew with the guilt he could still hear in Lilli's voice.

"Listen, you did what you had to back there. Demons, flying creatures, whatever—this whole thing is crazy. Crazy. I don't think any of us could have imagined how deep this thing really is. We still don't even know exactly what we're into now, so let's just try to make it home, regroup with the others, and figure this out. We're going to figure this out, Lilli. Don't worry."

As Liam watched her from the rearview, Lilli made sure she gave him the small smile he was looking for even though she wasn't at all sure that what he said was true.

Satisfied that Lilli seemed a little more settled, Liam shifting his attention to the shaken man directly behind him.

"What about you, Christof?" Liam asked. "Should we drop you somewhere or are you coming with us?"

Christof turned his weary gaze away from the blurred landscape outside his window to meet Liam's eyes in the mirror.

"Where else am I going to go?"

"This is absolutely insane! You said you tested Crane's DNA? How could that be right? How could there have been *no* evidence of an anomaly?" Eli paced frantically as he questioned Christof.

"I don't know," Christof stammered. "I was just Andreas' assistant. I'm not a scientist…"

"Perhaps you should sit down, Eli," Ngozi interrupted, noticing the deepening red in Eli's complexion. "This is a new species we're talking about here—something that can transform from an average-looking man to a 20-foot winged beast. I think we can put conventional wisdom aside for the moment.

"It's entirely possible, likely even, that we don't have the technology to detect whatever variant would identify him as something other than human. At least we know that these creatures are similar enough to our own kind to share some vulnerabilities. Lilli was able to kill one of these things. If she did it once, there's a chance that we can recreate the necessary conditions to do it again."

Eli knew Ngozi was right, he just couldn't stop pacing. Between the near-constant loop of grainy images on the news and his own mental replay of Lilli's account of what she'd seen and experienced, he was having a hard time reconciling the world he knew with all the evidence to the contrary.

Unlike Eli, his colleagues, Neva and Hasaam, were motionless where they stood in front of the TV. As soon as Lilli had finished her story, they turned on the news to find reports of sightings of the creatures Lilli had described all over the world. Occasionally, Eli noticed Neva writing notes as the news anchors speculated about events, but she said nothing.

Since Lilli, Joel, Liam, and Alessandra's return, the entire facility seemed to be divided into two groups—the smaller gathering that was listening in on the exchange between Eli, Christof, and Ngozi, and the larger crowd huddled in disbelief and worry around the TV.

"They're everywhere," Lilli whispered as she watched the sighting reports. "They've been here all along…"

Several heads nodded in agreement, but all eyes remained focused on the screen.

"Then why are they revealing themselves now? If they've been here all this time, hiding among us, then why are they suddenly willing to risk exposure?" Liam wondered aloud. "What do they gain?"

"Revenge," Lilli answered, turning towards Liam. All eyes turned to her. "Revenge for what I've done. For killing Crane."

"Not just you," Alessandra countered. "All of us. If what he told you was true about how he sees our power, then this is about more than just Crane. If these creatures feel the same way, then we have been reclaiming their access to our power ever since the first of us escaped. With Crane alive, maybe they thought they had a chance of regaining that control. Maybe that was the only incentive to keep themselves hidden. But now, with free Seers growing in strength and their leader gone, maybe now there is nothing to stop them from making us all suffer for what they believe was taken from them."

The sound of a woman sobbing into the camera drew their attention back to the TV. Though the woman spoke Farsi, a language no one in the room understood, the expression of raw terror and misery on her face was unmistakable.

The wave of nausea hit Alessandra so sharply, she barely made it to the bathroom in time with Liam rushing after her.

"Are you all right?" he asked as he jiggled the locked bathroom door handle.

"Yes. Go away," Alessandra groaned in between retching. "I'm just upset. I'll be out in a minute."

By the time Liam returned to the main room, Neva was writing furiously in her notebook as she tried to capture the interpreter's crude translation of the woman's account.

"They came from the sky! So many."

"How many?" the interpreter asked on the reporter's behalf.

"I don't know. I don't know. They had wings. Giant wings that blocked out the sun. They covered us in darkness. There was no time. No time. We ran."

"What happened to your daughter? Tell us what happened to your daughter."

The woman trembled silently for several moments before she could speak again, clinging to the embrace of an older woman who seemed to be the only thing keeping her upright.

"We lost her. She fell. They took her from us! I don't know. There was a light—

a bright, bright light outside the cave, and then they were gone. All of them, gone!"

"What do you mean, gone? How did she fall? Did they take her?"

"I don't know. I saw her, but I don't know. She...jumped. But it can't be this. Why would she do that? Why would she leave her family? She was a good daughter."

"I don't understand. Please, we need more information!" The reporter tried, but it was no use. The mother descended into her grief as the older woman holding her fended off the reporter's attempts for further questions with a wave of her hand and a stern look of warning.

As they began walking towards a small group of mourners, the reporter finally turned back to the camera in frustration. "What truly happened here…what happened to the young woman and the terrible beasts that descended on this remote corner of Afghanistan, we may never—"

"Jim!" the cameraman exclaimed as he saw the older woman return, reaching out her wizened hand to catch their translator's attention.

"She warned us, before they came. She saved us," she whispered to him intently in Farsi. "Seer. She was Seer."

There was a rush of commotion around them as Jim waited impatiently for the translator to convey her message, but by the time he understood enough of her message to ask what she meant, the old woman had disappeared.

Neva paused the broadcast then, and turned toward Lilli pensively.

Instinctively, Joel drew closer to Lilli, as they prepared to cautiously answer the barrage of questions they knew were coming.

"Do you think she was able to do what you did, Lilli, to defeat them?" Neva asked.

"I don't know," Lilli answered.

"She couldn't have," Liam interjected. "There's no trace of that girl. She could be dead, whereas Lilli is obviously fine."

Lilli kept her expression as neutral as possible as she avoided Liam's gaze.

"Well, regardless, our circumstances have changed," Neva continued. "I agree with Alessandra. There is more to this than just you, Lilli. There is a reason they are revealing themselves now. Whatever they are, they have chosen to exist in secrecy up until they first revealed themselves to us in Berlin—when they were chasing Liam and Alessandra. This started back then. I think our entire operation is a threat to them.

"What we know about the fallacy of the genetic marker, what we are trying to do with the Restoration Project, all of it threatens to destroy their ability to use Seers as a means of control—possibly forever. Who knows if the restoration process will be passed down genetically? But more than that, now they know that without the Luridium, Seers have the power to destroy them. Maybe the threat of the Seers and what we know is severe enough to make them come out of hiding just to ensure their survival."

The room was still for a moment as they each reflected on the pieces that Neva had put together before Jared spoke up.

"If we're the key to getting rid of them, then teach us, Lilli. Tell us how you did it," Jared urged.

"I'm not sure. I've never done it before," Lilli began, grateful that Liam had left the room to check on Alessandra again. "Ummm, I think it could—"

"Be dangerous," Joel finished. "Lilli's powers have always been unique. This was something even she wasn't prepared for. If we can really do this, then we will find a way to do it, but let's not rush into anything."

Seeing Liam reenter the room with a clearly weakened Alessandra, Joel continued, "As Liam mentioned, the girl in Afghanistan may be missing or worse. We don't want that to happen to any of us unprepared. So let's take a minute to figure out exactly what happened, with Lilli and in Afghanistan, before we make any moves to—"

Joel's voice was interrupted by the sound of Christof's cellphone ringing in a tone that was reserved for only one person. Embarrassed by the interruption, Christof fumbled with the screen before finally answering.

"Andreas?"

"So, you are alive," Andreas answered, sounding more irritated than relieved. "Did you find Crane? Where is he?"

It surprised Christof how pleased he was to deliver the news.

"He's dead."

There was a long pause before Andreas asked his next question. "Where are you?"

Christof's hesitation as he looked around the room confirmed Andreas' suspicions.

"I know you're with them. Give the phone to whoever is in charge. Tell them we want to talk."

CHAPTER 2: IN THE SHADOWS

Andreas could barely hear himself think as he sat barricaded inside the lower level of the UWO's facility in Geneva with the inane chaos of bureaucrats swirling around him. With the competing sounds of a dozen frantic conversations going on in seven different languages, Andreas doubted if anything was effectively conveyed to the people on the other end of the line.

The UWO, the Guild, the entire world was in a panic over the sightings of unidentified flying objects that seemed to have more in common with the depths of hell than outer space. As media outlets began reporting on the growing and seemingly random death toll caused by these creatures, the world barely had time to recover from the shock of discovering an entirely new species among them. Their motives, as well as theories as to whether or not they were newly arrived or had been hidden for centuries, were subjects of vigorous speculation. But as far as Andreas was concerned, none of it was worth the effort it took to listen.

He doubted that any of them knew more than he did—and he wasn't talking. Not yet.

So he sat as far outside the mayhem as he could, at the back end of a long conference table with his head pressed between his palms while he replayed his last conversation with Christof from a few short hours ago.

"Who is it?" Andreas had asked when Christof said he'd found a DNA match for Miguel's killer.

"You already know, don't you?" Christof accused. At the time, Andreas really hadn't known. He recalled feeling completely baffled by the mystery and the grotesqueness of Miguel's death.

But it should have been familiar, shouldn't it? Andreas chided himself now. *Maybe I didn't want to know.*

By the time he heard Christof tell Liam and Alessandra that Crane Le Dieu was responsible for Miguel's gruesome death, it felt true, but he couldn't reconcile the facts with the conclusion. It all seemed too fantastic for him to grasp until the first report came in of a large winged creature soaring above Geneva.

He knew immediately that the creature reported was Crane or some *thing* like him. Aaron's report an hour ago confirmed that Liam and Alessandra had been on the right track in assuming Crane was involved. Aaron had seen Crane, or one of his kind, take Lilli in Nice. Given what he had done to Miguel and others under his brutal hands, Andreas assumed that if Liam, Alessandra, and Christof were unlucky enough to find Crane, all of them, including Lilli, would be dead by now.

But what unsettled Andreas most out of all the strange occurrences of the past few hours was the question of why.

Why would Crane and whoever else was with him decide to reveal themselves now?

The potential of the answer frightened him like the dark corners in a room when he was a child. It wasn't rational to assume the worst of the unknown, but he couldn't stop himself. With no clear answers available, Andreas decided his best plan was to wait until Crane reemerged and say nothing until he figured out a way to use the knowledge he had to ensure either his protection or advantage.

After the first sightings, the UWO had followed standard lock-down protocol and called an emergency meeting with Guild leaders to determine if their Seers could give them any insight into what was happening and how they should mobilize their military resources to regain control of the situation. Anticipating that Crane would be unreachable, Andreas made excuses for his delay, expecting him to barge in and take over at any minute. But as the hours ticked on, Crane did not arrive.

In Crane's absence, the meeting descended into useless arguing quickly. The Seers offered no help. They could not see the creatures at all. Their ability seemed to be confined to merely predicting the death that would come from the creatures' presence as they swept across the globe. But their visions weren't clear enough to identify any specific information that could be useful in creating an effective evacuation plan. For those in the Guild, their vision was like watching a room full of burning people, with no context or detail to help rescue or prevent the tragedy. Even Aaron, the only member of The Red Order who was not dead or unconscious, was unable to provide any insight on how to contain the destruction the creatures would cause.

Early reports of confrontations with the creatures were not promising either. From the limited information that was known, it seemed that conventional aircraft and land weaponry merely slowed the creatures down, having no sustainable effect on their ability to wreak havoc wherever they chose. UWO leaders scrambled to deploy military resources as best they could, but without the Seers' capacity to predict the future, all the UWO's efforts were as good as a shot in the dark until a random report from Afghanistan offered an unlikely glimmer of hope.

As the only one not actively engaged in trying to solve the problems they faced, Andreas made out the words from the older woman on the television screen first.

"She warned us, before they came. She saved us! Seer. She was Seer," the older woman said into the camera.

At first Andreas didn't believe it. He got up from his seat and walked in disbelief toward the closest TV screen. He was about to ask one of the many assistants running around to replay the segment, but he didn't have to. The news station replayed the brief interview with the mother of a missing Afghan girl three times. By the time they were finished, Andreas was certain he understood what the older woman meant.

"Quiet! Everyone, shut up now! You need to listen to this!" Andreas roared.

His voice and tone were severe enough to capture the full attention of those in the room.

Exasperated, the Guild's Chairman turned toward the source of the outburst, "Andreas, if you're not going to help us, then—"

"I said, listen!" Andreas ordered. "Somebody rewind the segment from this channel. Put it up on the big screen." A young female aid Andreas had never noticed before quickly grabbed a large remote from the table and did as he requested.

"Andreas…" Deidra warned, but her voice trailed off as she began to listen to the broadcast. The aid kept it on loop until Deidra motioned for her to pause the replay.

"This can't be the solution," Deidra said in a low, shaky voice. "They'll never work with us. Not after what we've done."

"We have our own Seers. Maybe we could use them," the Chairman suggested.

"How?" Deidra countered. "They can't even see these creatures. The woman said the girl knew something *before* the event. At this point, even Aaron, with his enhanced capabilities, can't see them. It suggests that our Seers don't have something that they need, something that free Seers are able to access."

"Is it the Luridium?" another Guild council member asked. "We could take our Seers off the drug and see if that helps?"

Andreas finally spoke up. "It would take weeks of withdrawal to work through all the side effects, and after that, what would we do? Send them out and hope for the best? We don't know what that girl did. It could take our Seers months, years even, to master the powers Marcus and his group displayed in Chicago. And we still don't know if that would be enough."

"Years? We can't afford another week!" A member of the UWO shouted. "At this rate, we'll be extinct before the end of the month. If we want to regain control, we need to act now, with whoever can help us survive this."

"Do we have any idea where the Lost Seers are now?" the Chairman asked thoughtfully.

"No," Deidra replied as Andreas looked between them. "We've never known."

"We need to find them. After the world sees this, they will be expected to do something. If they come out and solve this problem on their own, our credibility, everything we've worked for will be lost. We need to find a way to do this without losing face," the Chairman concluded.

"This is crazy! Are you even hearing yourself?" another UWO member asked. "What will we do with our credibility when we're dead? Our people are dying! Do you understand that?"

Andreas took one last glance at the conference room doors, looking for Crane, before he spoke up. "I may know how to find two of the Lost Seers, if they survived."

The room went silent as the shock rippled through. Several people had questions, but Deidra got hers out first.

"What do you mean you *may* be able to find two of them? How?"

"They came to my apartment last night, looking for Crane."

"Who came to your apartment and why didn't you mention this before now?" Deidra asked, trying to control her anger.

"Until this moment, it wasn't relevant to our current situation," Andreas replied crisply. Deidra narrowed her eyes, but said nothing as Andreas continued. "Liam Knight and Alessandra Pino came to see me. Lillith Knight had apparently been kidnapped and they believed that Crane was somehow involved. They wanted to know where they could find him."

"And did they find him? Did you tell them where Crane was?" Deidra could hear her voice escalating, but she was too far beyond the desire to maintain a professional veneer to care. "Is that the real reason why he's not here? How could you not tell us this information?"

"I didn't tell them anything," Andreas snapped. "Christof did. He took them to the Morges."

"And where is Christof now?" Deidra spat.

Dead, most likely, Andreas thought, but he didn't dare admit it.

"Andreas, where..?"

"I don't know," Andreas finally answered. "I haven't spoken to him since he left."

"Well, call him!" Deidra said incredulously. "Maybe he can tell us where they are. We need to talk to them, to try to negotiate something, if we are going to figure this out."

Andreas pulled his phone from his jacket pocket and dialed Christof's number. No one was more surprised than Andreas when after the third ring, Christof answered.

"Where is Crane?" Andreas asked.

Christof's answer was not what Andreas had anticipated.

He's dead?

Andreas hid his shock behind a mask of stone as he tried to comprehend how anyone could have killed him, especially if Christof was right about Crane's ability to transform into one of the creatures he'd seen on the news. Inside, he felt tendrils of dread coil and tighten around his chest. Crane, with all his faults, had always been the one person Andreas could count on to fix any mess, even if he was the cause. He realized in that moment that, while he was often envious or even resentful of Crane dominance within the Guild, he never bet against him. Crane never lost, no matter what it took, until now.

Looking back at the image of the Afghan woman frozen on the television screen, Andreas understood that the balance of power had completely shifted out of their hands. And in this new world order of chaos, if they were going to survive, they needed to work with the Lost Seers.

He waited for several moments before he asked Christof to let him speak to whoever was in charge. Though he wasn't able to discern their words, the muffled voices he heard through the receiver were animated. When he finally heard a clear voice on the other end of the line, he recognized the British accent immediately. Andreas motioned for one of the assistants to begin a trace on his phone.

"So, you've seen the reports from Afghanistan and now you want to talk, is that it?" Joel began without pretense.

"Yes," Andreas said. "It appears that you may be the key to destroying these creatures and if that is the case, then we need your help. The world needs your help."

"You don't give a damn about the world! You only care about the parts that you can control and exploit for your own gain."

Andreas used his most placating tone as he proceeded to ignore Joel's accusations.

"Let me assure you that I speak for the entire UWO and the Guild when I tell you that we are willing to put our past differences aside to serve the greater good."

"Greater good, is it?" Joel scoffed. "Is that why you haven't put me on speakerphone? Does the Guild know that they've been led around by a demon this whole time? That even now, with all these people dying, you're still hiding that little fact to save your own ass? We see your intentions, Andreas. We know that there isn't a single one of you that we can trust to do anything other than serve your own interest."

Without thinking, Andreas began looking around the room to see if somehow he was being watched, but when he met Deidra's suspicious gaze he quickly refocused.

"Be that as it may, even if you could do what we suspect, there aren't enough of you to be successful on your own. You need our help, our resources. We would make anything you need available to you."

Joel was silent as he turned to face the people around him. With the exception of Lilli, the Seers were deep in their Quorum, feeding him insights as he spoke with Andreas while everyone else listened anxiously to the call. But where the Quorum's vision became clouded, Lilli's shone clearly in Joel's mind. Hearing her silent instructions, he nodded and spoke again into the phone.

"We will meet you tomorrow in Geneva. Three pm." And with that, he hung up.

"What did he say?" Deidra demanded.

"They don't trust us, but they will meet us here tomorrow."

With the exception of Andreas, the relief around the room was palpable.

"What's wrong, Andreas? This is a necessary compromise. Even you must understand that," Deidra said, taking some comfort in the fact that at last a plan was beginning to take shape.

"Crane is dead." Andreas said numbly. "Most likely killed by one of them. And this Joel seemed to be able to read our thoughts and intentions from wherever he was. I don't think there is any hope of controlling them, if we go through with this. They are more powerful than we realize."

"We'll worry about that after we've gotten rid of this threat. For now, we need to *make* ourselves trustworthy to secure their help," Deidra replied.

"Did we at least get a trace?" Andreas asked one of the assistants, all but ignoring Deidra's attempts at reassurance.

"No, sir," an older man answered back. "We never even found the signal."

●●··●●

The dim glow of the red emergency lights in the hallways made the walk back to his office feel ominous, but Andreas didn't mind. The eerie hue gave him more time to sort through his own thoughts and emotions. Andreas couldn't explain why he continued to keep Crane's true identity to himself. Part of him worried that he would be implicated in some wrongdoing since he had been Crane's partner for so long and had not known. But he also felt a sense of unfinished business. Despite his nature, Crane had been central to developing the Guild into what it was now – the most powerful and influential entity in the world.

Of all the institutions you could have built, why did you pick the Guild? Is this about the Seers? Did you know that they would one day be able to destroy you?

"Too many unanswered questions," he muttered aloud to himself as he unlocked his office door and closed it behind him. Even in the confusion of everything that had happened, his instincts told him that it was important to find these answers before anyone else.

Andreas was halfway to his desk before he noticed the girl from the conference room—the one who had replayed the segment on Afghanistan—stepping out of the shadows naked. Normally, he would have been amused at such an ill-timed attempt at seduction, except the expression on her face was anything but comely. Her eyes were predatory as she looked him over, sized him up. Fear raced across his skin like fire, and in that moment, he knew. Without a second thought, he turned to run, but she was too fast—inhumanly fast. She launched herself at him, immobilizing his body as she pinned his back to the door easily. As his eyes adjusted to the darkness, he watched in speechless horror as the smell of rotting flesh surrounded him, and the girl in front of him began to change before his eyes.

CHAPTER 3: ALLIANCE

With one powerful hand pressed against his sternum, the girl held him against the door as she bent down and began to tremble. Andreas could see the bones in her shoulders begin to shift out and break through her skin.

The stench from her body and the growing weight of what had morphed into a taloned claw on his chest were suffocating, but he couldn't make himself move. His knees trembled as urine trickled down his leg.

"Tama, leave him! Control yourself. You are here as a witness only."

Though Andreas could hear the deep voice, he couldn't determine the direction from which it came. His eyes, his senses, were helplessly glued to the sight in front of him.

But as soon as the words were uttered, the transformation he was witnessing seemed to stop and reverse itself—as if the scene before him was taking place in reverse, except for the weight of her claw, which fell harder against his chest, pushing the remaining air out of his lungs.

Finally, when her shoulders began to look more human, she stood raking her receding talons down the front of the suit he wore, tearing his clothes as she drew his blood.

By the time she removed her hand and stood to her full height, she appeared normal, though trembling slightly and drenched with sweat. Her teeth dug deep enough into her bottom lip to draw blood.

For a moment, Andreas felt feverish.

Did I imagine what I just saw? He thought, blinking several times at the young woman before him.

"This can't be real," he whispered shakily. "This can't be…"

"We are real. I assure you."

Startled by the proximity, the closeness of the voice, Andreas turned his head to find a large, muscular man just to his left. He stumbled away from him in a feeble attempt to escape before his legs buckled. The man caught him easily by the tattered collar of his shirt.

Suspended in the man's grasp, Andreas could feel his heart beating at a pace he knew he could not sustain. His eyes began to roll back until the man who held him upright shook him violently.

"Calm yourself," the man said in a voice that forced Andreas to focus. "We seek your help, but we offer much in return."

To Andreas' surprise, he felt himself carried, then lowered on to the soft leather of his desk chair.

"Their flesh is weak. You almost killed him," he heard the man say to the girl he called Tama. "Fetch him some water."

Andreas' heart began to slow as he took comfort in the distance his desk created between himself and the man whose eyes were not on him. For an instant, he considered reaching for his phone to call security, but then realized the thought was futile. There was no human who could spare him from what was about to transpire.

When Tama returned, she was fully clothed. She placed a glass of water in front of him, but Andreas found himself too afraid to reach for it. Instead, he stared warily between Tama and the man.

"Leave us," the man said to Tama. "You've done enough damage here." He waited until Tama had closed the door behind her to speak again.

"If we wanted to kill you, Tama would have already. Drink. I have business to discuss with you."

Andreas took the glass and downed its contents in three gulps. His throat was still parched, but he found he could breathe a little easier. For the first time, he looked down and noticed that there was blood on the shreds of his shirt—his blood.

He looked up as the man began to pour fresh water into his glass from a smooth, clear pitcher.

"Drink," the man said. "It's only a scratch...a warning."

Despite himself, need took over as Andreas reached for the re-filled glass with trembling fingers. Though she was no longer there, the girl's stench filled his nose.

"A warning for what?" Andreas asked when he'd emptied his glass and put it down.

"A warning of what will come to you if you do not honor our request."

Andreas breathed in deeply, trying to steady himself before looking fully at the man before him. He was a hulking beast, easily 6'5 with thick wavy hair that was dull with gray. His dress was slightly less than formal in dark pants and an overcoat, though he stood in an awkward, almost courtly manner with one arm behind his back. His face, his eyes, his entire countenance were ruddy and joyless, though he projected an unmistakable aura of power, if not quite authority.

But the man said 'if you do not honor our request,' Andreas reasoned.

The thought gave him a sliver of hope for his own survival. In his mind, "if" meant that there was at least a possibility of alternatives to negotiate, and Andreas knew how to negotiate. Andreas drew himself up as tall as he could in his chair and tried to ignore the smell of his own urine.

"What do you want from me?" Andreas asked.

"We want you to destroy the Seers, all those with the power to oppose you. Kill them and we will serve you, as we served Crane."

Andreas felt himself relax slightly at the ridiculousness of the notion.

"I can't destroy them. None of us can. If you hadn't noticed, we've been trying and failing miserably. You're the one with all the power. You and your kind are taking over the world as we speak. Why would you need my help?"

When the man did not answer, Andreas let the silence between them linger until he found the answer for himself in the way the man in front of him suddenly avoided his gaze.

"Afghanistan," Andreas began slowly. "This is about what happened in Afghanistan. They can kill you."

"Not all of them, just the ones who have the power to oppose you."

"They can kill us, too," Andreas answered cautiously. "A lot easier than they can kill you, I'd imagine. Why should we risk innocent lives— the lives of our soldiers—for you?"

The man's eyes softened then, as if he was about to smile, but he didn't.

"You, Andreas Menten, I have watched for a long time. You have never cared about your soldiers, much less innocent people. You destroy innocent people for a living. You trade their lives for the power you crave."

Andreas forced himself to look closer at the man in front of him. He didn't recall ever seeing his face before, but still. His palms grew sweaty as he gripped the armrest of the chair for strength.

"What do you mean, 'watching me'?" Andreas questioned, not quite managing to keep the trembling from his voice. "I've never met you before in my life."

"Not as you see me now. I took another form then," the man replied.

Andreas felt faint at the man's words. The impulse to yell, run or scream for help was primal – overwhelming. His life felt as short as his next breath, but he knew his only means of escape was to keep his mind focused on surviving. So Andreas continued, trying to regain the upper hand.

"If we are going to work together, I need to understand who you are."

"Understand me?" the man said with a scoff before shaking his head. "Crane always said that if you ever learned of our existence, you would act in whatever way served to benefit you most. He admired your consistency in this regard. He always believed we could trust you to do what was in your own interest."

"Crane told you about me?" Andreas asked.

"Yes, he spoke of all of you."

Andreas nodded, but didn't say a word.

"My name here is Saubos. I served the man you knew as Crane since before the time of your coming here on earth – from before the fall from Grace. After we came here, for countless years, we served him, looking for a way to become what we once were, but we could not recover our powers, our sight.

"But Crane did not give up. He taught us how to use our pain to control those around us. Crane decided that if we could not be what we once were, we would steal from you what you are. If God would not reclaim us, we would take this world for our own. Eventually he began to find them, others who had gifts like those we once had. They were not perfect, of course, but they were still beautiful. Still useful. This is how we lived until the Seers returned. Your science allowed us to harness them, break them and use them as we saw fit. Through their eyes, we glimpse the connection that was."

"Returned? What do you mean returned?" Andreas asked, struggling to put some context to the story Saubos told. "There is no history, no evidence."

Saubos' gaze hardened as his mouth turned into a sneer.

"Evidence? The evidence is in your blood. You are but broken pieces of your ancestors. Your kind gave up the knowledge of this history for the pursuits of this world—the hollow things we gave you."

Saubos' response still didn't make any sense, until Andreas thought outside the confines of the Guild. And then it clicked.

Joel, he thought. *The Restoration Project. If what Joel promised is true, then he would create a new race of people. People who could destroy them.*

Andreas spoke up cautiously, "But now the Seers have become too powerful...powerful enough to destroy you."

"Yes," Saubos said simply.

"I think I understand you now, but I don't see how I can help. Even if I could, why would I? Your kind is a menace. You show no regard for the order we have created."

"We show no regard for life we do not control," Saubos corrected. "If we can not control this world, we will destroy it. And you will help us, because the world they will create is not one you can control. There will be no benefit in it for you, only punishment."

Andreas knew that he was right, but he also doubted that an alliance with Saubos would ever be one he could fully trust.

"What assurance do I have that you won't kill me the moment the last of the Seers are dead?"

"You hold the key to the infrastructure we need to access their visions and maintain the world as we have ordered it." Saubos paused before adding. "You also have talents that we need. You can lead the Guild while maintaining our interests. Crane has groomed you, watched you. He always intended for you to succeed him. He valued your partnership very much."

The image Saubos presented in his mind was compelling. Whether his words were a manipulation or not, Andreas knew they were exactly what he'd always wanted—to be at the head of the Guild. Finally out of Crane's shadow, Andreas could lead the most powerful group in the world all by himself.

Feeling slightly more emboldened, he asked his next question.

"And what if I refuse?" Andreas asked.

"We will find someone else, after you are dead. You have certain qualities we seek, but you are not the only one. There are others who desire power as much, if not more, than you do," Saubos replied evenly.

Saubos' indifferent tone conveyed the truth of his words. Whether out of fear or ambition, Andreas knew that someone else would seize this opportunity if he didn't, so Andreas tried a different approach.

"I don't know if I can do what you want. I don't know where they are now."

"As I understand it, they will be here tomorrow," Saubos replied. "You have already brought them to us."

Andreas suddenly understood the reason for Tama's presence in the conference room.

"I didn't bring them. Joel named this place for our meeting. Surely they anticipate some advantage. If we set a trap, they'll see."

"Then we must give them a reason to come regardless. Use The Red Order to bring them here. Nina, Michael, and the others, I saw their concern for these people in Nice. Use it to bring them here. They will come."

"But won't they see you?"

"It is not likely, but it is a risk we are prepared to take. We exist between the physical and spiritual world. Most humans cannot see our true form unless we choose to reveal ourselves. Even your Seers cannot sense our presence in their visions. There is one who can see us, but she may have passed beyond us now. Either way, they will come."

"And when they get here?"

"We will destroy them."

"And what about the others, like yourself? Can you control them after it's done?"

"We are prepared to make sacrifices to return things to the necessary order. You can say that you captured us. Killed us off. You can say whatever you like. Once we have returned to the shadows, the world will be grateful and you will be more revered than ever before." `

Again, Andreas felt his own ambition, the desire to have everything he wanted swell within him. But his instincts also urged him to slow down and at least try to think through this improbable alliance.

"How many of you are there?" he asked, trying to distract himself from his own greed.

"We are many, but that is not your concern. We will restore order once we have eliminated our common enemy. Cooperate and we will ensure your power. Make your decision."

Andreas knew they had reached the end of their negotiations. Though he had no more leverage to stall, his hubris could not overshadow the enormity of the risk he was about to take. Even under the best conditions, he would always be beholden to them—these creatures he knew essentially nothing about. The thought was almost unbearable until he realized that it was really no different from the relationship he'd always had with Crane. Whether he'd understood it at the time or not, their partnership had always been a dangerous bargain between man and beast. So in the end, he asked the only question that would ensure his survival.

"How can I be sure this will work?"

"In this, we must trust each other. There is no guarantee. We must decide that we will not fail. We are the lie that creates the darkness."

Andreas didn't know what he meant, but with no other real options, it didn't really matter either way.

"What do you need me to do?" Andreas asked.

"Take Tama and bring her to The Red Order. That should be enough to set things in motion."

"Agreed," Andreas said, rising to extend his hand in an attempt to look like an equal partner.

Saubos hesitated for only a moment before extending his left arm as his right dangled at his side, bandaged coarsely at the wrist joint where a hand should have been. Andreas tried to keep the surprise of recognition from his face as he met Saubos's eyes.

"It is done," Saubos said as he squeezed Andreas' hand tightly.

CHAPTER 4: BAIT

Things had been strangely quiet in the Guild's medical facility for the past 12 hours. All the usual nurses who came to check on Pytor were nowhere to be found, and the new ones that did stop in at odd intervals refused to even look Aaron in the eye. When the last nurse who came by ran from the room when Aaron tried to ask a question, he finally realized that, like him, they were afraid.

Across the room, Nina and Michael lay still in induced comas that Crane had explained as "necessary" for their safety. But Aaron no longer believed that. His peers, his friends, his only family lay around him silent and silenced, and as the hours ticked on, he began to understand that the room where he sat had more in common with a prison than any medical facility in which he'd ever been. The evidence was all around that he needed to enjoy the gift of his own consciousness while he still could—before his fate was decided for him.

Sitting on the hard steel chair beside Pytor's bed, he traced the jagged scar that ran from the base of his palm all the way to the widest part of his forearm. Thinking back to the time when he got it, Aaron wondered if he would not have been better off if he had allowed the mob to kill him that day as they had planned.

● ● ‥ ● ●

As a child growing up in the mining town of Collinsville, Australia, Aaron had always been shy and unsure of himself. The youngest of six brothers, he seemed to be last in everything. Slow to learn and awkward, he was used to being uncelebrated, unseen, and uncherished. One of his earliest memories was of overhearing his mother as she joked with the neighbors that she didn't need another boy. "Especially not this one," she'd finished with a laugh. It was a lament she made frequently. If he was close by when she said it, she would give him a sound swat on the head just to prove her point.

His visions came earlier than most, in the form of dreams so powerful that he would sleep walk through the house describing events and people he had never met in languages he didn't speak. When he woke, he had no memory of what he'd said or why. Eventually, he'd scream so loudly in the dreams that the neighbors would hear. Aaron still couldn't say when the tolerance for his eccentricities turned from mild annoyance to suspicion and fear. He guessed that the shift had been too subtle for his 9-year-old self to detect, but all that changed two weeks after his 13th birthday.

The night before the accident at Abbott's Dock, Aaron had unknowingly described the coal ship's explosion in gruesome detail to his family and a handful of neighbors who had the misfortune of being unable to sleep through his rant. By the time the reports came in with nearly 50 men dead, word spread quickly that Aaron had predicted the event before it occurred. In the frenzy of grief and blame that followed, Aaron was targeted as the unseen cause of the disaster. A mob waited for him when he got out of school that afternoon. By the time his older brothers got to him, he was bruised and badly cut. But while they bandaged his arm tightly as they took him to the hospital, Aaron noticed that none of his family members offered him a single word of comfort. The looks of suspicion and distrust from his family members as the nurse cleaned and stitched his cuts hurt more than all the wounds he'd received from the crowd. At the time, Aaron had cried—begged for forgiveness—even though he could not even remember the vision that had apparently set all of these terrible events in motion.

By the time he returned home from the hospital, his family had received confirmation that his oldest brother, Thomas, had been among the men who died in the accident. Thomas had always been his mother's favorite, and from her bedroom, his mother's wails filled the house. But even though she was up all night, she never came to check on him.

Aaron developed an unrelenting case of insomnia as his own way of coping with his family's rejection, but it did not matter. No one forgot, and no one forgave. Worse, his entire family came under suspicion because of who or what they feared Aaron to be. It took less than two months for Aaron to decide to leave. On the day that he announced his intentions, hoping that his mother would talk him out of it, the expression of relief on her face was unmistakable. He took the bus to the next town straight from school, eventually making his way to a boarding house clear across the country where Crane found him years later, carrying news of his family's untimely death and a chance at a life more extraordinary than any he'd ever imagined.

●●··●●

Since joining The Red Order, Aaron had no reason to recall the sting of his mother's rejection until early this morning when Andreas requested Aaron's immediate presence in his office.

Aaron had never been to Andreas' office without the other members of The Red Order, and he couldn't shake the anxiety that dogged him as he walked slowly down the hall, fidgeting with the zipper on his jacket.

"Come in," Andreas commanded from behind his desk as soon as Aaron entered the office. "Close the door behind you and take a seat.

"Do you know what's happened?" Andreas asked the minute Aaron sat down.

Aaron had never known Andreas to be a particularly warm or friendly person, but the hostile edge to his voice still surprised him. His apprehension spiked as he stammered out the first response that came to mind.

"There has been no progress since yesterday, sir. The nurse says Pytor's vitals are stable, but I don't—"

"This isn't about Pytor!" Andreas snapped. "I'm asking if *you've* had a vision of anything…recently."

At a complete loss for words, Aaron could only stare back at Andreas with his mouth slightly open.

He doesn't know, Andreas guessed before Aaron found his voice.

"No, sir," Aaron finally managed. "We don't- I mean, I don't vision on my own, sir. We've never been taught to do that. We work as a team…" Aaron's voice trailed off as he watched Andreas' scowl deepen.

"Jesus Christ!" Andreas hissed as he grabbed the remote from his desk and motioned for Aaron to turn toward the large TV screen beside them.

As was the case on every station, the screen was filled with blurry images of flying creatures soaring through the air, followed by shaky footage of people screaming, running, then dying at the hands of beasts.

Andreas didn't miss the look of instant recognition on Aaron's face.

"Have you seen these creatures before?" Andreas asked.

"Yes… One in Nice," Aaron whispered as his eyes stayed fixed on the TV screen. "It took the girl. Lilli."

Aaron still had not dealt with all the things he'd seen at the train station in Nice. Tyrol turning against them, nearly killing Pytor, then bursting into flames while Lilli was carried away by something out of his childhood nightmares. When the chaos quieted, he fled to the safety of what was familiar, back to the Guild, hoping to have Andreas or Crane offer a sane explanation for what he'd seen and witnessed. But by the time he had returned, Crane and Andreas were gone. Knowing he was not allowed to discuss anything regarding The Red Order outside his group, Aaron remained silently at Pytor's side until he was summoned.

But, while Aaron watched the screen, Andreas' turned over the new pieces of information in his mind.

Could Crane have been there in Nice, as Liam and Alessandra suspected? Did he orchestrate the girl's kidnapping, and if so, why? Was the chaos upon them now a mistake or part of some larger agenda?

"Was it the same creature? Are you absolutely certain?" Andreas demanded, drawing Aaron's attention away from the TV.

"Yes, sir. The same...except the one that took Lilli was missing a hand. His right hand."

Andreas noted this detail, but kept pressing. "Can you see them now? Do you know where this creature is?"

"No, sir. I...I," Aaron stammered.

"Listen to me," Andreas said, leaning in closer. "These things are destroying us. Do you understand that? I need to know where they are now!"

"I'm sorry," Aaron tried again, "But I can't see them. I don't know how to."

Andreas let out a slow breath, trying to calm himself and regain his focus. "Have you told anyone else about this?" he asked while resting back in his seat.

Aaron shook his head fervently, but did not speak.

"Good. Keep it that way until I tell you otherwise. I have an emergency meeting with the Guild leaders to formulate a plan," Andreas said before adding, "It's clear you're useless to me without the others, but if I think of anything you *can* do, I'll let you know." When he was finished, Andreas waved his hand in dismissal.

Hurt and confused, Aaron got up and left without another word. On the way back to Pytor's side, Aaron lingered in front of one of the Guild's hallway TV, absorbing as much of the news story as he could without being noticed.

That was 12 hours ago, and in his silent vigil over Pytor, Aaron used the time to think about all the little connections that he'd missed: Tyrol's inexplicable closeness to Crane, Tyrol's clear familiarity with the beast that took Lilli, Tyrol's declaration that he would be one of "them," Nina's mistrust of Crane after Berlin which led to her removal from The Red Order and Crane's accusations that she and Michael had betrayed The Guild.

Aaron knew that Nina and Michael had been quoruming on their own ever since her reintegration into The Red Order, but up until this moment, he never thought of it as anything more than a brother/sister connection. Now he wondered if perhaps they had been communicating with The Lost Seers on their own.

Reluctantly, his mind conjured the image of Lilli suspended in the air.

Why did it take her? Aaron wondered. He knew that Lilli had always been an obsession of Crane's. *Was there somehow a connection between Lilli, the creatures, and Crane? And if so, where was Crane?*

Aaron looked over the still bodies of his colleagues and felt like he was seeing them clearly for the first time. The implications of his questions were frightening to consider, but with nothing but time within their confinement, Aaron didn't want to run from the answers anymore. As the only member of their group able to contemplate these issues, he sensed with growing urgency that it was his duty to find out the truth about their role within the Guild.

The events in Nice made him seriously question, for the first time, whether or not they were on the right side of this fight.

What if everything Crane told us was a lie, just like Joel and Nina said?

Looking around him, the answer seemed obvious. While Tyrol has tried to kill Pytor, Joel had saved his life.

We're trapped here, Aaron finally admitted to himself. *If we can't give the Guild the sight they need, they'll either make us into Quorum Seers, kill us, or…*

His train of thought was interrupted by the sound of the door opening. Aaron bolted upright as he saw Andreas, followed by a young woman he'd never met before, walk into the room and straight to the first bed within reach. His surprise immediately turned to suspicion as he watched the woman close off one of Michael's IV bags.

"What is she doing?" Aaron said in alarm. "Is she a nurse?"

"We're waking them up," Andreas answered firmly. "The Lost Seers will be here tomorrow and we need each of you to perform at your best."

"They're coming here? Why?" Aaron asked in disbelief.

"We need their help in eliminating the threat of these…new creatures that have arrived. They've agreed to negotiate a truce."

Aaron stared between Andreas and the woman for a while as she moved from bed to bed. Something didn't feel right about Andreas' words, but he couldn't figure out what it was until Andreas smiled and added.

"This is a time to come together, Aaron, to put aside our differences."

"I thought they were our enemies," Aaron asked cautiously.

"Things change. Sometimes the best solution is compromise," Andreas answered in a placating tone.

And in that moment, Aaron knew Andreas was lying to him. In all the time he had known Andreas and Crane, they had never been proponents of compromise in anything, and he didn't believe for a second that, with the Lost Seers so close, they would suddenly forget that stance now. In fact, if Aaron was being truly honest with himself, it was partly Andreas and Crane's absolute determination to defeat the Lost Seers that had made him want to be a part of The Red Order. It had been his chance to finally be the hero, to be first, to do something important. Or so he believed at the time.

"If we're putting our differences aside, why do you need us?"

"Because," Andreas answered. "You always bring your best assets to the negotiating table. It keeps everyone in line, and if they decide not to play along, you're our insurance policy that no matter what, things will go our way."

Aaron nodded as the woman finished her rounds and returned to Andreas' side.

"We should go," she announced. "In a few hours, we can check on them again and make sure they are ready."

Andreas nodded to the woman then turned back to Aaron.

"There is a security guard and a nurse just outside. Make sure you call the nurse the moment one of them wakes up. Your presence is very important tomorrow, Aaron, so get some rest. We will check on you again soon."

I'll bet we are, Aaron thought as he watched them leave the room and lock the door behind them.

You don't need us to defeat them, Aaron through in growing disgust. *You already know we can't. The only thing we're good for is drawing them out. We're the bait.*

Chapter 5: More than Us

"I can't believe we're actually about to walk into a trap with these people—again! Can someone please remind me why we're doing this?"

Vincent was half-joking, half-serious, and all bravado—as usual.

When none of the seven people riding with him answered, Vincent turned a pointed gaze toward Lilli, who sat quietly beside him in the front row of the van they had rented. Joel sat between them so that Vincent had to lean forward to see Lilli pressing her forehead to the cold glass as they swayed down the cobbled street that led to the Guild's Headquarters entrance. Vincent noticed that she held Joel's hand tightly as she looked out the tinted window with an expression that didn't give him any comfort. As if seeking confirmation, Vincent switched his gaze to Joel, who looked even more unsettled as he watched Lilli with a mix of helplessness, worry, and determination on his narrow face.

Shit.

Vincent checked the safety on his gun before setting it down on the rubber floor.

"All right guys, if you two are gonna act like we're driving to our deaths, then we need to turn this ship around—enough of the silent treatment. Either we bail or I need one of you to tell me what the hell is really going on here, right now."

The sound of genuine worry in Vincent's voice was enough to make Liam slow down a bit. The roads had been utterly deserted their entire way through Geneva. According to the news reports, there had been no sightings of the beasts in this area for almost 24 hours, but that fact only made Liam feel more on edge. There was no calm in the silence around them. He took it as a sign of what awaited them when they finally met with the Guild. He was also pretty sure that they were being tracked. Though he wanted to know the reason for the look on his sister's face as much as Vincent did, he knew this wasn't the time to ask. Alessandra, Lilli, Joel, Vincent, Maura, Tenzen, Ngozi, and Liam had all made the choice to come here, and no matter what new information Lilli saw in her visions, Liam understood that it wouldn't change what they came here to do.

● ● ·· ● ●

Joel's agreement to meet with the Guild was initially greeted with disbelief. For a few brief heartbeats after he'd hung up the phone with Andreas, the room was completely silent, but it didn't take long for people to begin voicing their objections.

"You can't be serious," Neva began. "You know this is a trap."

"Yes," Joel said simply, "but it's a risk we have to take to free the others. Andreas is right about one thing; if we are the key to fighting these demons, we will need every single one of us to do it, not just those of us who are free. To do this, we will need every Seer the Guild has. We can start with Michael, Nina, Aaron, and Pytor, and negotiate for the others…"

"And you think the Guild is just going to hand over the most powerful Seers in their arsenal, plus thousands more, their entire basis for control, to you? Joel, that's never going to happen. I don't know how you could even think it," Eli said incredulously.

"Not me, Eli. Us. And no, it won't happen all at once. But the Guild won't have a choice with the members of The Red Order, they will leave with us on their own. The serum Neva and Hasaam developed will help them, then we will negotiate for the others as soon as—"

"Negotiate?" Eli interjected. "You know better than even I do that you can't trust these people. They will use you, use all of you as a shield against these things… And if each and every one of you dies, they won't give a damn. They'll just start with a new crop of Seers and keep going. Don't throw your life away for nothing, Joel. There has to be another way."

"Eli," Joel said gently, "What has begun cannot be stopped. The Restoration Project has changed that forever. This was never about us. This was always about freedom for the others, for everyone."

"There's no guarantee that you can defeat these things," Hasaam said thoughtfully. "Lilli may have just gotten lucky. Remember, Alessandra was able to stop that man's heart with only her thoughts in Italy. But, just like Lilli, she doesn't know how she did it and it hasn't happened again. There is still so much we don't understand about how your powers grow and manifest. We haven't had the time to study what this means. Please, before you commit yourself to anything, we need more time to understand what happened with Lilli."

All eyes turned to Lilli then, waiting for a contradiction she could not give.

"I understand and agree with you, Hasaam, but we don't have time," Lilli said finally. "We have to try. This meeting is important. It will make what Joel has said possible. This is where we're meant to prepare for what's to come."

"What do you mean by that, Lilli? What's coming?" Eric asked as he came up beside Tess. The light still hurt his eyes, but he tried not to squint. He wanted to believe that if he was needed, he could be an asset to them.

"I mean that what you've seen on the news is only a fraction of their numbers. We've only seen the beginning of what they can do, and what they are prepared to do—against us. I felt Crane's rage. He's held it there for an amount of time we can't even fathom. They will have control over us or they will make us pay with our lives until we submit."

"Can you feel them now?" Alessandra asked.

"Yes, it's…" Lilli paused, looking for the right words, "a distant feeling, but it's growing."

"I feel it, too," Maura said, walking into the middle of the discussion. "While Joel was talking with them on the phone. It was the same sense I had at the train station in Nice, like a dark void, but spreading. Andreas is not a good man. His lies, his ambition…we know he will betray us, maybe even the Guild, but how, it is still difficult to see, difficult in the way that suggests that these demons are involved. We could not see clearly in Quorum. I hope they are not waiting for us in Geneva."

"They will be," Lilli said softly. "They will… I just hope we're ready." As soon as she said it, Lilli realized her mistake.

"You see this clearly, don't you?" Maura said, looking at Lilli more closely. "There is no doubt in your spirit. How do you see them clearly when we do not?"

"I…" Lilli began before willing herself to relax. If she was tense or lied, Maura would know. "Since what happened with Crane, I sense them more clearly, not always, but when I focus."

"This is a good thing, then," Maura said. "Like you said, it will help us prepare. Can you teach us how?"

"Yes," Lilli promised solemnly, "When I figure it out myself, I will teach you, if you want to learn."

Maura was about to ask why she wouldn't want to learn, but something made her stop. The pale lilac color that Maura had always seen in Lilli was pulsing and fading in and out of white—like nothing Maura had ever seen before. For a reason she could not name, she suddenly felt fear, for Lilli and for herself.

A secret, Maura realized. *A secret we are not ready to know.* The fear kept Maura quiet, as she studied Lilli more carefully in silence.

"How can we help? I want to help" Marshall asked, straining to give his voice the strength he lacked. Of all the recruits for the Restoration Project, everyone knew he suffered the most.

"You can't," Tess said as gently as she could, knowing that Eric was right beside her. "Not yet. Your vitals aren't stable yet, and I know many of you are still having symptoms from the treatment. I know you're anxious to see what you can do, but given what Lilli just said, this isn't the time."

"We will need you," Joel assured Marshall, "More than you realize, but not yet. For now, you need to rest and finish the treatments so that you can realize your full potential."

"So what's our plan," Liam asked, "If we know it's a trap. How do we make it out of there alive? Are we planning to somehow slip out under the radar or what?"

"No," Lilli said. "I can't see how many there will be, but I think we are going to have to fight our way out."

Liam frowned, wondering what help he could be, given what he'd seen with Crane, but he said nothing. In the end, it didn't matter. He would go and do whatever he was able to do.

Joel continued, "As I said before, the members of The Red Order will come with us. Some of them will be able to fight with us. Alessandra, we'll need your help with Pytor. He won't be able to come with us otherwise."

"How badly is he hurt?" Liam asked, already calculating the risks.

"The worst of the damage has been repaired through surgery, but no doctor can do what Alessandra can," Joel answered.

"But will she be in *danger*? She's already not feeling well." Liam said, growing more anxious. Alessandra tried to pull him back from his train of thought with a hand on his arm, but Liam wasn't about to let it go.

"Don't give me that look, okay?" he said staring down at her. "I know something's wrong."

Alessandra stared back at him for a long moment. She could feel Lilli's eyes watching her, wondering what she would say, but she could only tell Liam the truth.

"Nothing is wrong, Liam. I would not risk my life. There is too much at stake. Trust me. I will know when to stop."

"And we will help her," Katia chimed in with a wink at Alessandra to lighten the mood. "So who's going besides Alessandra? And Liam, of course?"

"Nothing is worse than before, Vincent. I just wish things could be different," Lilli said with a loud sigh. "It's just…disturbing. I don't mean to make you anxious." When she finally returned Vincent's gaze, Lilli wore a tired smile on her face. "Demons in my head make me a party-pooper, I guess. I told you not to sit next to me."

Joel laughed out loud in surprise as everyone else shook their heads and smiled at the welcome release of tension in the car.

Just up ahead, Liam could see the Guild's checkpoint. He counted five men standing at attention, watching their progression closely with guns raised and tracking their every move.

●●··●●

"If you're armed, we're armed," Joel said defiantly when the man at the checkpoint demanded that they unload all weapons before entering the building. "Andreas will authorize it. Call it in."

The man looked at him dumbfounded for a moment as he reached for the telephone. A minute later he was escorting them through the Guild's headquarters main lobby, with all the weaponry they'd brought with them.

"I know I'm good looking, but damn, they don't have to stare *that* hard," Vincent said jokingly as he took in the open stares around them.

"It's not every day you see the most hunted people in the world walk through your front door," Alessandra explained from behind him. "They've been taught to fear us, so they do."

They remained silent during the elevator ride down to the Guild's sub-level, until they were standing between the double doors of a large amphitheater-style assembly room. In front of them, a dozen men and women were waiting, seated behind an elevated, half-moon dais that was centered at the back of the room. The members of The Red Order stood to the left of them, looking fragile and frightened as they huddled around Pytor, who struggled to stay upright as he clutched the armrest of his chair with pale, sweaty fingers.

Joel and the others walked slowly down the center aisle with seating to the right and the left of their path until they reached the pit, where a narrow table with five seats and a pitcher of water was waiting for them. From their vantage point, the Guild members sat a good 10 feet above them, peering down with an undisguised sense of superiority.

With not enough room around the table, Ngozi and Vincent moved to the front row of seats directly behind the table. Before sitting down, Vincent took a moment to look around and confirm his count of the people scattered throughout the amphitheater, those in the far-back rows closest to the front door, as well as 3 others who stood in shadowed corners on either side of the room. When he was done, Vincent patted his gun then winked at a woman who sat behind him before taking his own seat a few rows ahead.

Beside Vincent, Ngozi was already shaking her head at the absence of glasses to accompany the water pitcher that stood high on the polished surface of the table before her.

The pitcher of water, this place, this meeting is all just a show, she thought in disgust. *They don't want us here. They hate having to ask for our help.*

The irony that the entire set-up was designed for passing judgment rather than reaching compromise was not lost on any of them, especially Liam, who took his time as he walked down the center aisle, purposely slow and last. When he finally reached his seat beside Ngozi and directly behind Alessandra, he'd counted the exits (besides the front door, there was only one to the left) and sized up and divided everyone beyond the dais into three categories: hired security (5), possible demons (3, maybe 4, because the girl by the entrance in the top left row seemed too unaffected by the tension in the room. Liam decided that she was a wild card that he'd try to shoot first, if he got the chance) and unsuspecting victims (6).

With nothing left to do but wait, Liam willed himself to remain calm.

This space was built to intimidate and confine, he thought. *The architects never imagined that, one day, the accusers might need to escape. We've got the best chance of anyone in this room of getting out of here alive.*

Their lowly position at the center of the pit gave them the greatest freedom for maneuvering, he reasoned.

The range of space and motion would give them an advantage that the men and women high above them would not realize until it was too late.

CHAPTER 6: THE MEETING

The Chairman of The Guild leaned forward to speak. Every Seer across from him was less than half his age, yet still he felt the inexplicable need to straighten his back.

Their eyes were piercing as they stared back at him.

Defiant, he thought, and though each of them could not have been more different in height and appearance, the focus in their gazes, the look of determination on their young faces was identical. He could almost imagine that he was looking at five different facets of the same person.

Do they share a mind, he wondered silently, *even out of Quorum?* The thought made him shiver and he let out a loud cough to hide the reflex from all the eyes he feared could see right through him.

"We are glad that you were able to put our differences aside and join us here today," the Chairman began in a forced, ceremonial tone. "Though it is unfortunate that you felt the need to come to this meeting fully armed, especially since everyone here understands that you pose a far greater threat to us than we ever could to you."

From behind the Seers, Vincent let out a loud snort as Joel stood to speak.

"Every Seer you hold against their will would disagree with you," Joel replied coolly. "Our presence here is already a show of trust that you haven't earned. We are not friends or allies, so there is no need to pretend. We're willing to work with you, to use our abilities, to fight the creatures that surround us, but only in exchange for the freedom of every Seer you have. That is the price of our cooperation."

Though the demand was not entirely unexpected, Joel's bluntness still shook the room.

"He can't be serious," someone muttered from the dais.

"That's impossible," another declared before Joel cut through their murmurs.

"We are serious," Joel answered. "Serious enough to risk our lives to come here."

At a loss for words, the Chairman turned hesitantly towards Andreas, hoping that he could manage to talk some sense into the foolish boy in front of them.

Andreas leaned forward in his chair, ready to take the reins at last.

"Joel, if I may call you that, we all want to come to a mutually tenable solution. That's why we extended this invitation to you, to see how we can work together. But you must also be willing to work with us. There are over 15,000 Seers currently under our care. Most are heavily dependent on Luridium. For us to release them all to you would surely overwhelm whatever infrastructure you may have in place, not to mention the fact that the transition from the Luridium is a slow, difficult process. I doubt that you could handle the responsibility of what you are asking. You must be reasonable." When Andreas finished, he folded his hands in front of him and gave Joel an indulgent smile, as if Joel were a child completely out of his depths.

"Reasonable?" Joel asked, squinting his eyes as if to see the people in front of him more clearly. As they stared back at him with somber, serious faces, Joel realized that most of them had no idea exactly how delusional they were. Only the woman he knew from Jared's visions as Deidra Pile had enough sense to eventually avert her eyes.

"There is nothing *reasonable* about what you do here," he continued. "The Seers here aren't under your care. They are prisoners. Slaves. Do you even remember the difference, or do you believe your own lies?" When no one answered, he continued. "And we are very aware of the withdrawal symptoms caused by the drugs you infect Seers with. We've already taken several Seers through the process successfully, as you can see for yourself."

Joel waited as their eyes found Alessandra, who stared back at them with an impenetrable expression. He then added, "You should not presume to know anything about our capabilities."

Undeterred by Joel's sharp response, Andreas continued with his line of questioning.

"I—we understand your position, but think of it logistically. To do what you're asking would be to create greater disruption to our society than there already is. As disdainful as our role within the world might be to you, people depend on us, especially in times of uncertainty. The food, healthcare, and other services we provide are needed now, more than ever. Your request threatens our ability to provide those things effectively."

Though Joel understood that Andreas' words were true, at least in the short-term, he also knew that whatever difficulty they encountered would still be better than the comfort of the Guild's oppression.

"People are ready for the truth. How hard it will be to confront that truth is in your hands, not ours. Unless you are unwilling to pay the price along with the rest of us—to give up your power to serve "the greater good," as you called it?"

Andreas could see that Joel was beginning to concede. *He knows there is some truth in what I've said*, Andreas thought. *To the boy's credit, he holds nothing back.*

Encouraged, Andreas prepared to move toward the second phase of his plan—feigning compromise, but the Chairman, whose anxiety had boiled over into indignation, cut him off.

"Don't you blame us for the havoc you will wreak!" The Chairman snapped. "These creatures, demons, god-knows-what, are threatening our very way of life, and you stand here, bargaining for a few at the cost of the many. There are over 7 billion people on this planet, and we are responsible for maintaining the very order they depend on! Do you honestly think it makes any sense to ruin billions of lives just to save a handful of people? You think only of the Seers, but we have the world to govern!" The Chairman bellowed.

Andreas couldn't decide if the expression on Joel's face was closer to contempt or the sheer disbelief people experience when they hear something so in conflict with reality that it makes them question their own senses. Either way, things were not going as planned. His entire goal for the meeting was to lull the Seers into believing that a sincere partnership was possible, even offering up The Red Order, after some perfunctory back and forth, as a show of good faith. After an agreement was made, Andreas would offer to escort Joel and the Red Order back to their quarters to gather their things. If they were as blind as Saubos believed, he would leave them there unsuspecting so that Saubos and the others could dispose of them quietly. But that seemed less and less likely as the Chairman let his insecurities run away with him.

"Perhaps we could refocus," Andreas tried, but Joel's steady voice was already muting his words.

"You don't maintain order, you exploit it. No one gave you the positions you hold. You made them up amongst yourselves—in secret— because if you'd done it in the light of day, no one would have given them to you. You have no right to govern anything."

Joel delivered his words with such cool finality that the Chairman's face began to turn a blotchy red.

"How dare you! How dare you come in here and speak to us that way!" He seethed.

Andreas chanced a glance at Tama and was surprised to find her on her feet, staring at him with a cruel gaze from the back of the room. When she had warned him earlier that morning that if he did not handle the situation, she would, he had not given much thought to what she could mean beyond his own death. But something about the way she stood at attention as her gaze shifted across the room made his stomach plummet in fear. Andreas began to feel dizzy and the sensation made him even more afraid. He looked across the dais to his colleagues and realized with certainty that they were all going to die if he didn't get a hold of himself and the entire situation, now. As he glanced up to pull his microphone closer, he noticed that Lilli was staring at him with a look that went right through him.

His throat constricted around his words as her gaze seemed to peel him open.

For a moment, there was nothing. No sound, no chatter in his mind beyond one pulsating thought.

She knows.

My God, she knows.

He had to close his eyes to break the connection. He could hear the Chairman's voice becoming shriller with exertion. In a panic, Andreas grabbed his microphone.

"Excuse me, Mr. Chairman. Mr. Chairman, please, if I may—" Andreas interrupted. The Chairman was about to wave him off before he noticed the anxious, almost pleading looks of his colleagues. These were not silent nods of approval. *Far from it,* he realized. They were afraid, and he had gone too far. Wiping the sheen from his forehead, The Chairman met Andreas' glare and nodded for him to take over.

Andreas took a deep breath as all eyes returned to him.

I have to make this happen, he thought with focused desperation. *We have to get out of this room.*

He cleared his throat.

"Joel, I believe what the Chairman was trying to say was while we may not meet your criteria of what is right, you must realize that we are *necessary,* at least for now. I knew your father, Marcus, for many years and I'm sure even he would have—"

Up until that moment, Joel had found it strangely effortless to maintain his calm demeanor, but the mention of his father caught him off guard. The anger came so fast that the words rushed out before he had a chance to think them through.

"Don't you *ever* say his name again! Not to me. You have no idea who he was. I watched you take him away after you murdered my mother, right in front of me! So don't tell me what he would have done when all of YOU are the reason he is dead now!"

Joel had never felt so out of control of his power in his life, not even when he didn't know how it worked. At least then, whatever he might have done would have been an accident. If he acted on the sudden hatred in his thoughts, if he burned each of them alive slowly, like he wanted to, it would have been entirely on purpose.

He could feel the heat of his power rippling through his body so strongly it made his legs tremble. Every ability he had to shape, gather, and break the elements around him was focused, ready to attack and defend him from the source of his rage. All he had to do was extend his hand to set his thoughts in motion.

Instead, he looked down and pressed his hands flat onto the table's surface, fighting to keep himself from acting, until he felt Lilli slow her mind enough to be in sync with his again. When she took a deep, calming breath, he felt it. It was all he needed to pull himself back from the edge.

The room was silent when he looked up towards the dais again, but all eyes were set not on the renewed calm of his face, but on the faint tendrils of smoke that were drifting up from the place where Joel had burned and shaped the wood of the table into a mold of his hands.

Deidra was the only one who had the courage to speak.

"I think we need to start again," Deidra said in a rush as she tried to pull her focus away from the impression of Joel's hand on the solid mahogany table that had been smooth and level a few short seconds ago.

"Please allow me to apologize for our insensitivity and the way this meeting has been conducted up to now. My name is Deidra Pile and I, we, need your help. I don't know if I speak for all my colleagues here, but I can assure you that I am under no illusions about what will happen to all of us if we can't secure the cooperation of you and your…team. I am prepared to pay whatever price I need to pay to get it because I am sure that none of us will survive without it. Now I understand that for you, what we have done to…your family, your kind, is unforgivable. I have my own reasons for being a part of this, but I won't argue them with you. I am as guilty as you see fit to make me, but as despicable as we all may be to you, I urge you to think of the larger costs—all the innocent people who will suffer if we can't come to some kind of accord.

"We are dealing with a situation that we are wholly unprepared and unequipped to handle. You've made some very serious demands, and I want you to know that I take all of you *very* seriously. I understand that you would not have come here if you were not serious, but before we talk about how we meet those demands, we need to know if you can stop them. Do you know what these things are or what they want from us, and most importantly, if we give you what you want, are you sure you can kill them?"

"Deidra!" the Chairman shouted. "You do not have the authority to come to any agreement with these people!"

"Maybe not," Deidra said, staring him down coldly. "But I won't let your pride ruin the one viable chance we may have to survive. This is not a game, Paul. Like it or not, we need these people, or we're all going to…"

Deidra's voice was drowned out by the sudden clang of two heavy doors slamming shut, followed by the sound of locks clicking and sliding into place from the outside.

Deidra shielded her eyes from the overhead light to get a better view of the front door, but it was impossible to see clearly. All she could make out was a tall, broad figure that had his back to the room.

"Excuse me, sir, but this is a private meeting. You'll have to leave," she called to the man, but he made no move to turn around. She was just about to call for security when she heard Andreas's hoarse whisper from where he sat beside her.

"Oh God! Not here."

The first scream came from a woman Deidra could not see. Her line of sight was blocked by Liam's figure as he stood up and turned around with a black semi-automatic rifle in his hand. The motion of his body was so fluid, Liam seemed to have stood up, aimed, and fired all in one continuous motion, before her ears had even registered the sound of gunfire. His target was clear as the bullet caught the neck of a slender, unfamiliar young woman who was standing at the back of the room.

Deidra was so stunned she could not look away as the woman clutched her neck, trying to stop the rush of dark fluid that spilled from it. For one endless moment, the room seemed to stand still as Deidra's shock turned to confusion then horror as she noticed that the woman did not simply fall, but rather leaned forward, baring her bloody teeth before letting out a ferocious growl that shook the room.

Chapter 7: Nothing as it seems

Before her snarl could reach its full pitch, Liam and Vincent unleashed their weapons on the woman and three other men who had begun moving toward them.

All around them, the room erupted into chaos, with people in the audience leaping and stumbling over their chairs to get away from the gunfire and the fear of something much more terrifying. Some headed towards the beckoning of Joel, Maura, and Tenzen, who tried to draw them closer to the back exit, while others ran to the sidewalls hoping that the security guards could offer protection, most of whom seemed frozen in place.

One security guard managed to get on his walkie-talkie and call for help only to have his hopes dissolve into terror when he heard the sound of his rescuers screams as they were battered and broken against the double doors that trapped him inside. After that, he huddled on the floor with the rest of his colleagues and those he was paid to protect. From the far back corner, only one guard held firm as he shifted his gun nervously from left to right, unsure of exactly who the enemy was. In a split second of panic, he decided to take down the man who shot first, firing his gun at the back of Liam's head.

●•⋯•●

There was nothing random about each person who decided to come to Geneva to meet with the Guild. Each had a specific role to play in what they needed to achieve. Lilli's primary role within their mission was to use her enhanced abilities to open up the blind spots that were created by the presence of the demons in their future. By using her expanded vision, she hoped to pinpoint their location within the Guild headquarters and give the Collective any insight she could gain on exactly how to fight them effectively.

The task would have been simple if she was willing to give in to the process that ached to take over her being. But she couldn't, not yet. Instead, she found herself fighting both sides of a war to maintain her physical self while simultaneously stretching the boundaries of her abilities. Still, even with the strain of her internal battle, Lilli's mind was alive with a heightened awareness and focus she could barely contain.

When Liam insisted on coming with them, Lilli wasn't worried. She could see the important role he would play in securing the safety for those who found themselves caught in the crossfires of their battle. She also knew that every Seer among them would do whatever they could to keep him safe and where they might fail, she was confident that she would not. In addition to the raw power she was struggling to control, she knew that her own ability to sense and process information was now beyond even Joel's capacity. So it took her almost no effort to divide her attention between her primary focus and stopping the bullet that headed towards Liam.

Before she had fully formed the thought, the bullet halted in mid-air and hurled backward in the direction from which it came. At the last moment, Lilli altered its trajectory so that the bullet exploded into the wall just above the guard's head. Instinctively, his gaze shifted past Liam to the Seers and found Lilli staring back at him with a look that chilled the sweat on his body.

He's not the one you need to be worried about, she whispered into his mind. Her voice pulsed and echoed through his thoughts so loudly that he dropped his weapon, pressing his hands into his temples in a vain effort to squeeze her out of his mind.

But before he could yell out for her to stop, Lilli shifted her eyes away from him and her voice was gone.

The entire incident happened so quickly, Lilli was surprised to find that it had not even registered within the Collective. But when Lilli looked to her side, she saw Maura risking the briefest glance in her direction before helping a woman free her ankle from between the seats and crawl to safety.

Behind Lilli and Joel, Alessandra and Ngozi had made their way past the scattering of frantic people to the members of The Red Order, who were hunched protectively around Pytor in his chair as he slumped over, breathless with pain and fear.

"What's happening?" Pytor managed through gritted teeth.

"Shh," Alessandra answered while lowering him on to the ground. "Don't worry. I'm here to help you. I need you to relax." Gently, she laid her hand on his tender, swollen stitches.

Not as bad as Berlin, she confirmed, though the stitching and synthetic materials the surgeon had used to repair his body would make it harder for her to heal him.

Beside her Ngozi wiped the sweat off her palms and turned to Aaron.

"Roll up your sleeve," she said curtly. "We need to disable your tracking signal."

Aaron looked between Ngozi and Alessandra skeptically, but did not make a move.

"Do as she says. We don't have time," Alessandra ordered. "If you want to come with us, all of you need to do this now."

Understanding dawned on Michael, Nina, and Aaron then, and they rolled up their sleeves hastily as Ngozi prepared the syringes.

Over the sound of screaming and gunshots, Alessandra closed her eyes, shutting out the noise in order to give herself a quiet space to focus on Pytor's wounds. She was about to begin when she felt Aaron's hand grasping her shoulder.

"It's a trap," Aaron grunted, as Ngozi jammed the first of two syringes into his arm. "I don't know why, but they used us to get to you."

"We know," Alessandra said quietly as she continued to do her work. Pytor held her hand tightly as he began to feel a strange heat building in his chest.

While Michael, Nina, and Aaron focused on Alessandra, Ngozi worked as fast as she could to administer the serum that Hasaam had modified for the unique brand of Luridium they used with The Red Order. Though the serum was effective, it was not without its own side effects. As soon as the last dose was administered, she set the timer on her watch.

"If we're lucky, we'll have at least 10 minutes before the seizures start," Ngozi muttered while packing up her medical supplies. She was so focused on not screwing up her first "field assignment" that she didn't realized she'd spoken her thoughts aloud until it was too late.

"Wait. What did you say?" Michael asked sharply. "I thought you said this would disable our tracking signal. What the hell did you do to us?" Three pairs of angry eyes bore down on her.

"It will," Ngozi replied quickly, projecting her voice over the chaos in the room so that they all could hear her. "The first shot was to disable the tracking signal by introducing a new bonding agent that will alter the electrical charge in your system from negative to positive. Unfortunately, the sudden change in polarity will likely throw your neural impulses off balance for a moment, which may cause seizures."

Their eyes grew wider as she prepared to give them the good news with her most reassuring smile. "That's why I gave you the second shot—

for the seizures. Don't worry, the chance of any permanent brain damage is almost negligible."

"Gee, thanks," Nina said as she rubbed her arm.

While taking in Ngozi's poor bedside manner, another disturbing thought crossed Michael's mind.

"Are you even a doctor?" He asked doubtfully.

"I'm a paleontologist," Ngozi answered defensively.

"You mean, you study dead animals!" Aaron said in a panic.

"It...surprisingly relevant—" Ngozi began before Alessandra interrupted their argument to address Nina.

"Head over to the others. They will need your help," Alessandra said.

"With what?" Nina asked as the room suddenly went silent. Alessandra seemed to be oblivious to her question as she, Michael, and Aaron looked around. The walls were littered with bullet holes. Chairs and people were scattered around the room haphazardly, with some hiding, some wounded, and some dead. To her left, Nina could see the half a dozen Guild members who had not tried to escape, cowering in fear behind the dais. The only people standing were Joel and those who came with him. In contrast to the others, they stood tall, each appraising the four corpses that lay still on the floor. By the amount of blood and number of bullet holes on the bodies, it should have been obvious that they were dead, yet no one seemed confident enough to move.

"Huh," Vincent said smugly as he looked between the bodies. "That wasn't too hard. I think you were wrong this time, Lilli. I think we got 'em. They're dead, right?"

Lilli had already warned them that these creatures could not be killed by conventional means. Liam and Vincent's weapons were only meant to slow them down, to buy them time to administer the serum and save as many people as possible before the real fighting began. But, Vincent liked to believe he could beat almost any odds.

Looking around, Liam could understand why Vincent was so confident, but he wasn't convinced. With his rifle ready and reloaded, Liam took a step towards the large man slumped against the double door entrance who was missing his right hand. Instantly, he remembered Katia's account from Nice and the description of the man she maimed. Seeing the cut now, he knew the man should have bleed to death in less than a minute. But instead he survived and lived long enough to kidnap his sister.

"They must be weaker in their human form," Liam announced before backing away.

"I'll say," Vincent replied, his grin spreading wider, "That's what you get when you use the razor rounds. They don't just penetrate, they shred," he added proudly.

Slowly, heads began to peak out over the tops of chairs and tables, with a glimmer of frightened hope in their eyes.

"Is it over? Are they gone?" One of the older Guild members asked.

Maura shook her head, while Lilli answered aloud with her gaze turned toward the ceiling.

"No," she said absently as if listening, waiting for something.

"What is it?" Joel asked. Then he heard it, the slightest crack in the concrete ceiling above them. Though Lilli's thoughts were moving too fast for him to follow, her instincts were very much in sync with his. He could taste the bitter adrenaline in her mouth at the same moment she did. A second later, the ceiling split in a jagged fault line that ran through the center of the room.

CHAPTER 8: FALLEN

G et down! Stay Down!" Joel yelled as the ceiling burst open under the weight of four massive beasts descending on them.

Debris fell all around them as each demon jumped down in quick succession, landing with a force that cracked and buckled the ground beneath their feet. Floorboards, tables, and chairs that had once been bolted down erupted from the ground, leaving fragile bodies suspended among them in a sickening instant of silence before everything came crashing down.

The dais, which up until that moment had acted as a haven for the Guild members, slammed into the wall behind them, trapping some, while crushing others.

Yet Liam had not hit the ground. Like Vincent he was suspended almost horizontally in the position where he had begun to fall. The sounds around him were strangely muted as his eyes darted across the room to find Alessandra exactly where he had seen her last, hovering over Pytor underneath a shimmering cocoon of blue-white light that surrounded her and Ngozi. And for a moment, he lost himself in the simple gratitude that she was alive and safe from all the madness around him.

In there, no one can harm her, he thought, as his body began to float down.

It was then that he saw Lilli and Joel, with their arms extended towards himself and Vincent. He realized then that he was being carried gently in the shimmering light of Lilli's force field. Nearby, he could see Maura and Tenzen using their own shields to protect themselves from the debris. For one brief instant, everyone he cared about was safe and protected.

But it couldn't last.

One by one, Liam was jolted back to his senses as Lilli's shield unfolded from him and he felt the hard ground meet his back. Sound came next as screams of pure terror flooded his ears followed by a deafening screech that the beasts surrounding them seemed to make in unison. It was equal parts anguish and fury. Listening to it, Liam could only imagine how enraged the demons must have been with their inability to inflict harm on the Seers, but the cloud of dust and debris around him was too thick for him to get a clear enough view of their faces to confirm his suspicions. Smell and taste came last as he coughed down his first mouthful of putrid air.

By the time Liam closed his hand around his mouth, he could just make out the figure of the Guild's Chairman as he suddenly rose from his prostrate position on the floor and took off in an insane sprint toward the front door. The third beast, which was closest to Liam and the front door, sneered, baring his grisly teeth as the Chairman attempted to rush by. Anyone in view could see what was about to take place and screamed their warnings, to no avail. The beast waited for the Chairman to get close enough to just grasp the front door handle before he reached out and caught him by the face with one enormous claw. The Chairman's screams were muffled and brief as the beast twisted the Chairman's head like a bottle cap, severing it from his body. Crazed from the victory with the Chairman's body still dangling in its claws, the beast sought out its next victim, resting his eyes on Liam.

And in the instant it took for their eyes to meet, Liam could feel his entire body turn to ice. Suddenly incapable of movement, Liam watched helplessly as the beast discarded the Chairman's body and charged towards him.

With every step the beast took towards him, Liam saw his own death approaching. Suddenly, Joel eclipsed the beast from Liam's view as he rushed in between them. Stunned that he was still alive, Liam watched as Joel extended the palm of his hand toward the beast. Dark particles seemed to materialize from the air itself, forming a dark cloud that hovered and spun just above Joel's outstretched hand. With a flick of his wrist, Joel sent it forward in a whirling tunnel towards the beast in front of him. The black dust went straight into the demon's chest, burrowing into its skin before exploding, catapulting the demon across the room.

"Liam, get out of here!" Joel shouted as he turned his attention to the second demon.

The sound of Joel's voice finally unlocked his body. Suddenly able to move, Liam scrambled to his feet, heading toward the first cover he spotted—a large overturned wooden table that had somehow been thrown to the other side of the room. Behind its relative safety, Liam took in the scene around him. In front, the Seers had taken up three distinct positions in teams of two, forming a virtual wall of protection for the people behind them, which happened to include Alessandra, Pytor, Aaron, and himself. When Liam looked behind him to find the exit sign glowing red above his head, he was shocked. Before the ceiling came down, he had been standing much closer to the center of the room. Lilli or Joel had moved him to this location on purpose.

Turning his attention back to the chaos, his eyes darted from one unbelievable scene to the next. Liam had seen a lot of incredible things over the past two years, but nothing that came close to what he was witnessing now—people who were much more than humans battling winged beasts that should never have existed at all. As he felt the seconds tick by, he realized that he would have to force his mind to orient itself to the impossibility of everything that was actually happening.

With more focus, he turned to his right and watched as Michael and Nina used a bright blue energy that looked like lightening to push a creature two times their combined size into a wall without even touching it. The beast thrashed back at them, even as it howled in pain.

To his left, Maura and Tenzen appeared to be attempting to restrain the beast they were fighting in ribbons of light that seared its skin on contact. And in the middle, Lilli and Joel stood back-to-back, surrounded by four beasts. They moved together in a constant motion, hurling and throwing one while dodging and fending off attacks from another. To Liam's relief, though the beasts around them were cut, bruised and bloodied, Joel and Lilli seemed unharmed. And closest to him was Alessandra, working intently and safely inside a force field of light with Aaron nervously standing guard.

But for how long? Liam wondered anxiously.

With the dust settling around them, Liam once again counted the number of demons they were fighting.

We put 4 down when we started, then another 4 came from the ceiling, so why are they fighting 6? Liam studied the creatures Lilli and Joel were fighting more closely until he found the answer he was looking for. One of the larger beasts that was lunging toward his sister was missing a hand—his right hand.

Shit! They're waking up!

Liam looked around frantically, unsure of what difference he could make in the battles being waged around him until he saw the bloodstained face of a young man dragging himself towards Liam on his belly.

Suddenly, Liam understood what he needed to do. The man was no more than 150 feet away. Liam realized he could get to him and others who might be wounded, but first he would need some help.

"Stay where you are. I'm coming to get you," Liam shouted towards the injured man before shifting his gaze to look for the one person he knew wasn't engaged in a supernatural battle.

"Vincent!" Liam shouted because there was no point in being quiet. "Vincent, can you hear me? We've got to get them out!"

In response, he heard coughing and a faint groan to his left. Liam got on his knees and crawled towards the sound while dodging fallen debris.

"Vincent?"

"What is that damn *smell?* It's killing me, man. Killing me. Don't they have deodorant in hell?"

Liam couldn't help but smile.

"Are you all right? Are you hurt?"

"Yeah, I'm ok. Just a little banged up, but I'm fine. Have you seen my gun?"

Liam looked around the floor until he saw the braided strap of a rifle covered in dust.

"Yeah, I got it. We need to move. They're waking up. We need to find whoever's still down and *keep* them down, then get these people out of here, before we're completely surrounded."

Vincent pushed his own makeshift barricade aside. To Liam's relief, Vincent's eyes were fully alert as they met his gaze.

Liam gathered the wounded together as best he could while Vincent worked the interior of the safety zone that the Seers had created for them to make sure that no other beasts made the transition from human to thing. When he found Tama about to crawl to her feet, he fired until his pants and shoes were splattered with the blood and tissue. Vincent wanted to draw closer, convinced that he could finish the job, but he resisted his pride, choosing instead to back away and returned to Liam.

"I found two of 'em," he said while trying to breathe through his mouth. "They're down now, but who knows for how long."

Of the five people Liam was able to rescue, only two had the strength to move on their own. Most were badly wounded and Ngozi carried the only medical supplies they had.

"Ngozi!" Liam yelled out. "I need the bag!"

He didn't know if she could hear him from inside Alessandra's cocoon or not, but he had to try. If he wasn't able to treat them soon, he would be forced to leave them there. But with Aaron's help, Ngozi got Liam's message and made her way over to the tiny corner that had become Liam's triage center. Together, they bandaged, patched, and splinted as best they could.

"How long before those guys fall apart?" Liam asked Ngozi while gesturing towards Michael, Nina, and Aaron.

"I gave them the injections 4 minutes and 10 seconds ago. We've got 6, 7 minutes tops before at least one of them has a seizure. If that happens, we'll have to carry them out of here and given what we've already got on our hands…" Ngozi's eyes flitted over the wounded as she lowered her voice, "We're not going to make it."

"Aaron!" Liam called.

Hesitating for a moment, Aaron left his guard beside Alessandra to run over to Liam.

"Do you know the way out of here from this exit?"

"Yeah, I think so," Aaron replied.

"We have a van waiting outside the main entrance. I need you to lead these people there. Can you do that?"

"Yeah, I guess so, but what about Pytor and Alexandra? I shouldn't leave before she's done."

Liam didn't have time to correct Aaron's pronunciation. He needed to convince Aaron to get moving.

"I've got them. We'll be right behind you, but we need you to go, right now!"

Aaron looked suddenly ill as he nodded his head. But Liam could see the fear in Aaron's eyes. If there was any other way, Liam would have tried to take the wounded himself, but he knew they needed someone stronger than he was, someone with powers he didn't possess. Liam grabbed Aaron by the arm and spoke to him in a voice that conveyed the urgency of the situation.

"There may be more…creatures out there. These people will need your power to protect them. Can you do that?"

Aaron took a second to quiet his mind and calm his stomach. This was what all his training in The Red Order had been for, he reminded himself. Crane had once called them gods among men. He wondered if that sentiment included demons. Looking back at Lilli, Joel, Michael, and Nina fighting for their lives, he had to believe it did.

"Yes," Aaron said as confidently as he could.

Vincent and Ngozi organized the group while Aaron opened the exit door and stepped tentatively outside. Behind him, the sounds of fighting and destruction seemed amplified against the still calm of the exit hallway. For a moment, Aaron stood in awe of the contrast that was so welcoming and completely out of place at the same time.

"Get down!" Aaron heard Vincent shout, but his distraction made him slow. Aaron turned around to come face-to-face with one of the beasts flying right for him with an expression of sheer rage on his face.

Frozen in place in the doorway, Aaron watched helplessly as one of the survivors with minor injuries shoved aside a wounded man she was supposed to be helping to the exit. Faster than anyone would have believed, she ran towards the door, inadvertently placing herself right in the demon's path. From behind, the demon opened his mouth as the air became filled with a putrid smell. Aaron watched in horror as the demon's bottom teeth grazed the back of her skull. The woman reached out for Aaron as she screamed, her eyes wide with the realization that he would be the last thing she ever saw. But just as the beast began to dip his head and close his jaws, Liam caught the woman behind the calves and pulled her down, jerking her body out of its mouth.

Aaron was now directly in its path, unable to move or think of anything beyond the hot stench rolling towards him. The beast got within inches of his face before a flash of white light flickered around its neck like a noose and yanked it back.

As the demon beat its wings in protest, Michael and Nina hurled its massive body back into the room and up into the ceiling, causing a new storm of debris to descend from the floors above.

"You can do it, Aaron! Lead them - now!" Michael shouted.

Michael's words stunned him. *Me? I can't,* he thought, before looking down to find his hands glowing with a blue white light that he'd hadn't noticed before.

Could I have stopped the beast? He wondered. A moment ago, it had not occurred to him to even try, but now Michael's words rang in his ears. *Lead them.* Looking back at Michael and the other Seers who were fighting to give them a chance to survive, he was determined not to make the same mistake again.

"Aaron!" Liam shouted from where he was helping the woman he'd saved up from the ground. "Are you up for this!"

Aaron wasn't sure how long Liam had been standing there waiting for him to speak, but when he looked up from his palms, he was finally sure of his answer.

"Yes. I'm ready," Aaron said simply as he turned and stepped into the hall.

●●·· ●●

Aaron led them out. The most able-bodied of the survivors followed him at a safe distance, carrying their assigned wounded between them. The woman who had abandoned her charge before now had a broken nose from the fall that saved her life and appeared to have no desire to leave her group again. Vincent covered the rear behind Ngozi, making sure that nothing followed them out. Liam stayed behind, promising to follow them as soon as Alessandra was finished with Pytor, but Vincent knew there was at least one other person that he wouldn't leave without.

The hall was wide and winding as it curved through the solid concrete walls of the building's lower level so that you couldn't see more than a few feet in front of or behind you. But, while sound was muffled and light was scarce, smell travelled unhindered. From 10 feet ahead of them, Aaron got the first whiff and stopped in his tracks.

A cold sweat broke out all over his face, but when he looked down, his hands were a bright blue as if lit from within by fluorescent light. He held up his palm to tell the others to stop and turn back quietly. Though he could not hear the demons approaching, their stench grew stronger with every second he stood in place. Behind him the others shuffled and ran as fast as they could. Only Ngozi looked back as she saw Aaron still standing in place with his arms stretched out and glowing blue.

Chapter 9: Only a little brave and a little strong

Almost a minute had passed since Aaron and the others had turned the first bend in the hallway and vanished from Liam's sight. The silence that stretched between where he stood and where they might be felt comforting.

At least some of us will make it out of here, he thought, as he watched Alessandra from across the room. Shouldn't she be done by now? He wondered as he moved to close the door and make his way to her. The door was almost shut before he heard the sound of pounding feet.

"What if the door's closed?" Liam heard a woman ask through labored breaths.

"Then we'll blast it open," Vincent replied as his shaggy, overgrown hair became visible.

Swinging the door back open, Liam was about to ask what happened before he realized he didn't need to. There would be only one reason that they would have turned back. He rushed out to help and noticed right away that someone was missing.

"Where's Aaron?" He asked, but no one had the heart to answer.

"Aaron!" Liam called from just inside the door. When he didn't get an answer, he turned to Vincent. "Give me your gun."

"Stay where you are," Liam heard Aaron say. His voice sounded distant, yet strong.

Determined, Liam thought, but it didn't matter. Liam knew what Aaron was up against and he was fairly sure that Aaron had no chance of surviving on his own, even if he was a Seer. From what he had observed of the fighting going on around him, the members of the Red Order had a long way to go before they developed their gifts to the level of any Seer in the Collective.

With every intention of disregarding Aaron's request, Liam was hoisting the strap of Vincent's gun around his neck when the exit door suddenly slammed shut, locking them in from the outside.

●•·•●

The stench surrounding him was so intense, he could taste it at the back of his throat. He took only two small steps back then planted his feet, determined to go no further. His stomach threatened to convulse, but he held every muscle in his body tight, willing his entire being to conform to his command.

"Show yourself," he whispered. They were so close now that the smell was overpowering.

And then they stepped out from the bend in the wall that obscured them from his sight. There were two of them. Though they were much smaller than the ones he had seen in the conference room, they still towered above him, more than eight feet tall with their wings high and folded in behind their backs.

"You are only a little brave and only a little strong," the one closest to him mocked as he sniffed and looked Aaron up and down. They had split off from each other to begin circling him slowly.

It's true, Aaron thought without an ounce of doubt, *but I only need to be strong enough to save them.*

"Serve us and we will not harm you," the second one hissed from behind. "Do not waste your gifts fighting us."

Aaron wanted to think of a smart response but he couldn't. He'd never been good at that sort of thing with the bullies at his school, and he wasn't any better at it now. Then he remembered something Michael used to say when they were training as new recruits to the Red Order.

"It's not what you *say*, but what you *do* that makes people take you seriously," Michael had said as he demonstrated his superior powers to the group. At the time, his words seemed obvious and boastful, but now, Aaron could see the real truth in them. Action took the type of courage he had never had, until now.

Aaron shifted his body so that his arms were parallel with each of the creatures that circled him before. He opened his arms in a gesture of surrender. The blast of energy that came from each of his fingertips were like knives heated in a blazing fire, cutting and burning into their marred, ruined flesh.

While the creature to his left managed to spin away from the blast and escape with only a series of cuts across the right side of his face, neck and shoulder, the beast to Aaron's right was not so lucky. His attempt to move away from the sudden attack caught him in the back, leaving deep gashes on his left shoulder while severing most of his right wing. In agony as it fell to the ground, the creature let out a shattering scream that made Aaron's eardrum split in two. His hands flew up to cover his ears as his eyes shut tightly against the pain, making him unable to see the first demon aiming its claw at his left temple.

The blow knocked Aaron face first into the opposite wall before bouncing off and landed on his back. For a moment, Aaron couldn't see. His only awareness consisted of an excruciating ringing in his ear and the awful smell that seemed to get worse as he gasped for air.

Then he felt his body being yanked up by his neck and all his senses returned. The right side of his jaw and neck were slick as blood trickled from his ear, while the left side of his face throbbed with pain. The creature dug its claws into Aaron's neck as he held him high against the wall.

The demon whose wing Aaron had clipped was still screaming in pain, but he couldn't hear him as well as before and realized it was because he had gone deaf in his right ear. Aaron felt a strange calm wash over him as he looked into the red-green flecks within the black eyes of his captor. He knew he would not need his hearing much longer.

"You are a fool to think that you could defeat us!" The creature in front of him seethed.

"You're just angry because I hurt your friend," Aaron heard himself say. To his utter surprise, he realized that he was smiling.

"Hurt? You know nothing of hurt. Our pain is eternal. We have endured more suffering than you could ever comprehend."

Aaron found himself nodding as he took in all of the beast's scarred and twisted features. And in some newly discovered place, he found that he truly did understand.

"You are the face of hate," he whispered hoarsely as the beast tightened his grip.

"No," the creature sneered. "I *am* hate."

Yes, Aaron thought with a sense of satisfaction. *Yes, you are, and I have never hated anything in my life. You have never lived inside me.*

Slowly, Aaron raised his hands and placed them on the creature's forearms. To his surprise they shimmered and glowed brighter than ever before.

The creature began to convulse at Aaron's touch, but he did not let go as the brilliance began to spread through Aaron's arms and chest. Both Aaron and the creature watched in fascination as the light grew bright enough to see through Aaron's clothes and eventually though the creature's own skin.

From outside the circle of light they shared, the second demon began to shout.

"Let him go, Dhikkāra! You will be lost. Let him GO!" He begged before hobbling away from the scene in a panic.

But Dhikkāra would not—could not—listen. The pain he felt was worse than anything he could recall, but it was also cleansing in a way he had never hoped to feel again. Tears welled in his eyes as the remnants of his skin began to peel away, turning him into something almost-new for the first time in millennia.

Let him take you, too, Keder, he thought. *Let him take you, too.*

And as the pain grew, he surrendered to the light in the boy who was not so brave, and not so strong, yet powerful enough to do the one thing no one else could: give him peace.

Aaron's smile was the last thing to dissolve into light as his mind extended out of all limitations. In a final exhale he released his energy into the space that could no longer hold him as it consumed everything in its path.

●•··•●

From inside what was left of the assembly room, things had gone from bad to worse. No matter how hard they tried, Liam and Vincent could not get the exit door to open. Ngozi did her best to keep the survivors huddled together as the space around them disintegrated. Looking up, she could see at least three floors above them due to the gaping hole that was widening in the ceiling. Through the dust and debris, she could easily make out more lifeless bodies scattered around the room, broken from their sudden descent from above. But what made her body shake with fear was not the death that surrounded her or even the shock of witnessing demons in their midst; instead, it was the exhaustion on the Seers' faces as they battled four creatures that simply would not die. The change in them from even a few short minutes ago was clear. Each of them was drenched with sweat, their clothes torn and dusty. Joel had a large gash across his arm that had not been there when she'd left to escape with the others. She watched him now as he rolled away from a demon who had managed to side-swipe him with one of his wings even as Joel had knocked him to the ground. Joel got to his feet quickly enough, escaping the mouth of another beast who tried to close in on him, but he had a limp in his gate, and his eyes were squinted as if trying to push away some pain from his consciousness. Lilli was only slightly better. With no blood that Ngozi could see, Lilli still looked no less in pain. Maura and Tenzen both had angry bruises on their exposed skin, yet were still making their way over to Michael and Nina, who had propped themselves up against a wall. With blood running down his forehead, Michael fought wildly, throwing streams of electricity haphazardly as one beast prepared to close in on him. By his side, Nina looked around dazed and unseeing with her hand outstretched as she tried to project her shield.

Fear gripped Ngozi's chest as the sudden certainly of death welled up inside her.

Not now. Get ahold of yourself! These people need you, she told herself as she felt panic begin to take over. She hadn't had a panic attack in years, not since she was a little girl locked in a dark closet by the children who bullied her at school. Every time, Joel would come and pull her out before the anxiety could swallow her whole. But he was too busy fighting his own demons to save her now. Frantically, she looked around for someone, something to hold on to, and found Alessandra helping Pytor rise to his feet.

Help us! Help them! She wanted to say, but her throat wouldn't work.

To her utter relief, Alessandra seemed to sense her fear. Their eyes met briefly as a terrible scream of pain rang out from somewhere outside their space. Alessandra looked up then, past Ngozi's pleading gaze, to see Liam desperately trying to open the door in fear of what might be happening to Aaron. Ngozi's fleeting hope began to dissolve as Alessandra's eyes suddenly widened in terror.

"No, Liam! No!" Alessandra shouted just before something large crashed into the door that separated them from the hallway. The impact sent Vincent and Liam tumbling to the floor. Ngozi turned from Alessandra to the door and found Liam and Vincent trying to get back on their feet just as another crash split the paneling on the wall, sending splinters of wood and plaster everywhere.

Horror overshadowed Ngozi's panic as a claw reached through a wide crack in the wall. She sat frozen as the being attached to it let out a scream that was strangely human in its agony. Through the opening she could see a bright light filling the hallway. As the light grew brighter, it consumed the claw that was suspended in the wall until it was barely an outline of dark inside the light.

And the room fell silent in a surreal moment of perfect peace.

Alessandra's shoes made almost no sound as she ran towards Liam and the small group of survivors in front of her. With her body, her mind, and everything else she could spare, she extended her energy out, bringing them fully under her protection as the light became blinding and Aaron's energy shattered the wall around them.

CHAPTER 10: PRECIPICE

Lilli's mind had been racing from the moment they entered the cavernous space of the Guild's conference room.

This is a tomb, she'd thought as she catalogued each face in the room without her eyes ever leaving the ground. When she did finally lift her gaze to find Joel staring at her curiously, it startled her to realize that she had not actually *looked* at any of them. Her mind had perceived them from some place outside her body.

She had not known that she was doing it, that she *could* do it, and the thought alone terrified her. If the powers she possessed were not under her control, how could she keep herself from succumbing to them?

How much longer can I keep this up, she wondered, as she tried to rein herself in again.

The constant struggle to stay whole, together, while her mind wanted to expand into everything was like a dull ache in her bones. On the one hand, she needed to use her expanded ability to keep them safe and help them survive what they had to face. But every time she used her new ability, it pulled her further away from the living, from the physical to the spiritual realm. The distance between the two felt less than paper thin. In front of her loomed a split-second decision that she could not make until the time was right or there was no other choice.

Keeping the balance would have been all-consuming, except her mind could now handle so much more.

As the fighting started, she found she could direct each of them in what to do as she viewed their positions from every vantage point. She could monitor their vitals and their energy levels as well. And if they need more, she could lend them parts of herself—perception, energy, insight—just as she did with Liam in Chinatown, without their knowledge. All this she could do while fighting her own battles.

But the limitations of the human body were real, and no matter how they tried—how she tried—they could not escape the exhaustion of fighting six beasts who had every physical advantage over them. Despite the toll it took on each of them, she knew it was easiest for Joel and herself. Not only did they have the strongest abilities among them, but they also had the greatest understanding of those powers. Joel could feel the slow dance of a billion particles of matter moving around him. Intuitively, he understood their relationship to each other and how they could be used to create and destroy simultaneously. For Maura and Tenzen, it was similar, but not as organic. They understood their connection to the energy that existed within and around them. They could focus it, harness it and project it outward, but they could not restructure its composition as Joel could. Nina and Michael had the least awareness of themselves or their gift, which made them the most vulnerable among the Seers.

As the fighting went on, Lilli could see within each of them the need for more oxygen, replenished nutrients, and above all, rest. If it were not for their innate rapid healing abilities they would have died already from any number of human frailties—cardiac arrest, internal hemorrhaging, or they would have simply passed out from fright.

But we were made for this, Lilli realized. *We are stronger for this.*

Still, this can't go on much longer, she thought, turning her attention on Michael and Nina. In the future, she had seen them as powerful beings, but looking at them now, worn and frightened against the wall, it was hard not to doubt the truth in her vision.

She knew that the Luridium and their lack of familiarity with their gift were mostly to blame for their limited ability, but there was also doubt and fear that got in the way of the power they needed to access. Lilli was just about to send them her vision of them in the future to encourage them when another presence unexpectedly entered her mind.

Up until that moment, nothing that had taken place had been a surprise to her. The more she tested the limits of her abilities, the clearer she was able to see, even with the obstructions the demons caused in her sight. But the sudden awareness of a familiar consciousness hovering in the same space as her own was unexpected.

Aaron? Lilli thought, feeling an immediate connection to the racing of his thoughts.

How can you resist this? Aaron asked as they shared the rush of their heightened awareness.

I have to…, Lilli replied.

Yes…they need you, Aaron answered. *But I must go.*

Before she could ask him why, his thoughts began to blur in her mind, moving too fast for even her to comprehend.

Aaron, she called out. But he was gone.

Her perception stretched out, trying to find Aaron, but he was beyond her reach. Instead, from outside the conference room she heard the panicked shrieking of an animal running in fear for its life.

He's running towards us, she thought as she tracked its progression to the spot where her brother stood leaning his full weight against the exit door, still trying to save a man who no longer needed saving.

Instinct told her to move in Liam's direction, but that didn't make sense. There was too much distance and at least one demon standing in her way. Grateful that Alessandra was nearly finished healing Pytor, Lilli sought out her next best option.

Alessandra, Lilli called. *Get him.*

From inside her shield, Alessandra heard and understood immediately. Confident that she had taken the precautions needed to ensure Pytor's health and protect her own, Alessandra began helping Pytor to his feet.

The room seemed to stand still for a moment as the beast trying to escape Aaron's power crashed into the wall. When his claw finally broke through, Lilli saw the light. As those around them stared in confusion, hers and Joel's mouths hung open in wonder.

"Is that what we are?" She whispered.

"Yes," she heard Joel say beside her. "That is what we will become."

Lilli turned to him and smiled inside the shield they shared as the entire back wall exploded in around them.

Before the dust could settle, the room rang out with a series of screeches and roars as three of the demons fled in fear, while the others rose from the debris of the explosion, enraged by the demise of their kin.

Maura, Tenzen, Michael, Nina, Joel, and Lilli folded together in the center of the room as three massive beasts began to circle around them.

Lilli and Joel exchanged a quick glance before Joel spun out from the group. The two demons to his right stepped back as he approached, watching a bright blue ball of light glow and crackle as he seemed to draw energy from every corner of the room. Because they were smaller than the demon to his left, he attacked with his right hand first, hurling them back and through the front wall with all his strength. The impact left them limp and silent on the hallway floor, though Joel had no way of knowing for how long. Unwilling to waste any time trying to figure it out, Joel shifted his body to the demon on his left. In his exhaustion, he hadn't really focused on the demon he would be facing until he stood right in front of him, but he couldn't have asked for better motivation. In fact, he couldn't resist the smile that pulled at his lips when he realized that, unlike the others, he knew the grotesque features before him from the Gare Centrale Thiers station in Nice.

This is the one who took my Lilli, he thought, drawing his eyes quickly to the missing right hand. Joel's rage was like a shock of energy to his system, propelling him forward as he prepared to choke the life out of the thing in front of him. With both hands extended, Joel propelled the beast high into the air before holding him there, with a cloud of grey black particles that wrapped around his neck like a vice.

Jesus, Lilli thought, as she turned from the scene to face Maura and Tenzen.

"Get them out of here. Take Michael and Nina and go!"

"No," Tenzen insisted. "We need to stay together."

Look at them. It was all Lilli needed to say. Maura had seen Michael and Nina's lights fading for the last few minutes, but hoped that they could hold on until they were all out safely.

"I know you see it, too," Lilli urged Maura, but Maura only shook her head in response, too conflicted to speak.

"The last time I left you, you almost died," Maura said finally.

"I won't die…" Lilli began before Maura looked at her sharply.

Do not lie to me, she spoke silently. *I know you know what will happen.*

Lilli looked directly into Maura's eyes, chastened by Maura's honesty. *She deserves the truth*, Lilli reminded herself.

I will not make that choice, Maura. I promise you.

Hearing the truth, Maura's eyes softened before she reached out, giving Lilli a brief hug before helping Nina to her feet while Tenzen put his arm around Michael.

There was no time to look back as Lilli turned around to hear Joel grunt in pain. Suspended above Joel, Saubos thrashed his wings furiously, catching Joel on the side of this arm that was already wounded.

"Put him down," Lilli shouted as she watched the veins in Joel's temple pulse and twitch with pain he had been hiding from her up until this moment.

"I can hold him," Joel grunted, "Get them out," he said, his eyes flashing towards the dais. "She's still trapped."

Lilli nodded, as she focused her power on him to finally break through the mental barriers he'd put up to shield her from his pain. Understanding it fully for the first time took her breath away. Even with his body working frantically to repair his wounds, the tears to his ligaments and small fractures in his bones made it excruciating to stand, yet he was upright, tall as a reed as he fought. Without hesitating, she gave him every ounce of healing power she had.

She could see the impact it had on him immediately. The muscles in his arms and legs stopped trembling and the gash on his arm began to shrink as the flesh wove itself back together. They had a job to do, a mission that was more important than both of them, but it still took all of her strength to turn away from him and finishing what they had come here to do.

She was running towards the dais, stretching her hand out to move it aside, when a smaller demon she had not fought before leapt in front of her, blocking her path.

The urge to speak the thing in front of her into oblivion was powerful. She knew without a doubt that she could do it. The words were on the tip of her tongue, but Lilli held them inside. The last time she had done that, she had opened up a door that threatened to suck her right through it. Lilli stopped short, planting herself in place.

"Move," she said simply "And I won't hurt you."

The creature before her scowled and sneered, but said nothing before turning around. At first, Lilli hoped she would flee, but the thought died as she watched the creature suddenly smash the dais in two with her fist.

"No! Lilli yelled as she rushed forward, but it was too late. The beast had already flung part of the dais aside to reveal Andreas and Deidra huddling together on the ground.

Deidra began to scream as Andreas silently shook with fear.

The creature let out a snarl as it reached for Andreas.

"I should have killed you when I had the chance. You failed us, you miserable—"

The voice was strangled but clear as it rang out from behind them.

"No, Tama…not him!" Saubos croaked before falling silent.

She hesitated for a moment before shifting her reach. Tama snatched Deidra up in her claws quickly, but by then Lilli had grabbed her firmly by her other arm.

"Put her down," Lilli said in a voice that reverberated throughout the room.

Tama shrieked, unable to pull away from the girl whose skin began to give off the faintest glow.

"This one would have led you to us," Tama hissed. "She would never risk her life to save yours."

"That's not true! Please! Please!" Deidra begged.

"Silence," Tama snapped back as she tightened her grip around Deidra's throat.

"You will let her go," Lilli said more calmly as Tama's arm began to glow like Lilli's.

"What are you doing?" Tama shrieked. "You cannot harm us! You are nothing!"

"Now." Lilli replied as the feeling of warmth and light beckoned her. Tama released Deidra from her grasp against her will, consumed with the sound of Lilli's voice in her head. She could feel a burning sensation travel up from the point of Lilli's touch to her arm and throughout her chest. The panic that was evident in Tama's expression as she felt herself being consumed from within was not mirrored in Lilli's expression. As the light grew between them, Lilli was filled with an inexplicable joy and peace. She felt herself beginning to expand outward as if the air from her lungs could fill the world. Her sense of her own self seemed to fade away in the openness that was now rushing in to take its place.

But somehow within this great expanse, she heard something that anchored her, a sound from which she could not turn away.

"Lilli!"

The sound was a voice. Calling a word, a sound that was important.

"Lilli, come back to me!"

The voice. A man's voice. His voice.

"Lilli!" He screamed from behind. Strong arms wrapped around her torso. The light died around her as she could feel her body begin to take form again, becoming solid where he touched her so that she could feel the beat of his frantic heart right through her spine.

"Lilli, I'm here. You are *here* with me." Joel's voice was fierce as he squeezed her tightly.

The air was sour as she sucked it in and opened her eyes. When Lilli released the demon from her grasp, Tama dropped to the ground, twitching once before taking her last breath.

Lilli's next exhale was filled with blood as she leaned forward into Joel's embrace, coughing and gasping for air.

Joel lifted her in his arms and ran toward the gaping hole that had been the back exit door, barreling past Liam and Alessandra who had been standing nearby, watching the entire scene take place.

By the time Joel reached the hall, everyone was behind him. The hallway was clear except for the bodies of three men who lay charred on the floor. But Liam maintained his focus, sweeping the rear to make sure they weren't followed. But more often than not, he found himself helplessly turning around to watch Alessandra as she kept pace with Joel with her hand placed on Lilli's forehead. He didn't want to see it, but the evidence of what had happened—of what was happening—was everywhere, in the strange bodies on the ground, in his sister being consumed in a light he didn't understand, and in the terrified expression on Joel's face as he cradled her in his arms.

By the time they made it to the van, Liam knew he was screaming, barking out orders as he watched Nina and Ngozi try to pull a convulsing Michael into the van, but he couldn't hear the sound of his own voice. All the chaos around him seemed to move in silence. On the front row of seats, his sister lay on his wife's lap while Joel hovered over her, kneeling in the small space with Lilli's blood glistening on his hands and face.

Vincent took the wheel as the gunfire erupted from behind, with Maura projecting her shield around them just long enough for Liam to close all the doors and climb into the van. As they sped away with a swarm of guards chasing them, Liam swung open the back door and used Vincent's gun to fire mercilessly into the darkness that was coming for all of them as surely as the tears running down his face.

CHAPTER 11: IN BETWEEN

The feeling of clinging to life was worse than death itself.

Lilli could feel her insides knitting back together angrily, in protest for being ripped from bliss. Only her mind and heart understood the reason why she had to stay, the rest of her body didn't give a damn and let her know it.

As Alessandra worked to heal her body, Lilli tried to focus on her breathing, but the intake of air felt hollow, as if the oxygen was running over her cells rather than through her body, unanchored within the chamber of her lungs.

"Lilli, can you hear me? We're here, Lilli. We're all here. Stay with us."

Joel's voice was a whisper as he knelt down beside her in the van. Though she couldn't manage to turn toward him, she could see him clearly from a vantage point high above his left shoulder. From this place, she observed her resurrection and all the pain it caused with an unshakable calm. She could see Liam swallowing his own grief as he fought to keep them from being followed by the Guild. She watched Tenzen cradle Maura gently in his arms as she cried for all the sorrow that she could see and feel around her, while his own tears sank into the thick robes of her hair. Beside them, Ngozi had turned into the scientist she was trained to be, patching, administering, and assessing with a methodical precision that shielded her from all the feelings she couldn't process.

"Stay with us," Lilli heard Joel say again, but his voice seemed distant now even though he hadn't moved an inch.

The realization that it was she who was moving farther from him made her heart jolt with fear.

Focus. Lilli's voice echoed in her head as she forced her awareness back into the confines of her body. Slowly, she could feel the air funnel through her bronchial tubes, pushing their molecules past tissue and blood vessels as living things do.

It was only then that her eyes turned to Joel's bloodied face. He stared back at her, with eyes that were sharp and clear enough to guide her the rest of the way home while Alessandra coaxed her bones back from fragments into strong, solid things.

Lilli didn't close her eyes until she was sure she would be there when she woke up.

Liam stood in the middle of the room, his face filled with anger and disbelief.

"So, why can't you fix this? You guys can do everything else, why can't you fix this?"

Ngozi, Hasaam, Neva, and Maura stared back at him—feeling as hopeless as Liam did, but trying not to show it.

"Liam," Neva began quietly, "I don't think that anyone can stop this. Her entire cellular structure is...unstable. I think her collapse, her distress is being caused by her attempts to stop a chain reaction that has already begun."

"What does that even mean? What are you saying?"

Neva pressed her lips together and averted her eyes.

The prolonged silence between them seemed to drain Liam's courage to face the answer to his question. He began to shift his weight anxiously where he stood until Hasaam finally stepped forward, raising a hand to place on Liam's shoulder in reassurance. But when he saw Liam flinch away at the mere suggestion of his touch, Hasaam thought better of the gesture and lowered his hand.

He needs the truth now, Hasaam told himself. *Not my comfort.*

"You know our bodies are made up of trillions and trillions of atoms," Hasaam began, watching him closely. He knew that Liam was a very smart young man, but he also knew that at this moment, Liam was not thinking logically. He needed to proceed with caution.

"When an atom splits, it releases an incredible amount of energy due to a chain reaction that accelerates as the atom expands outwards. Once it begins, reversing that process is—*should* be—impossible, like putting a bomb back in its canister after it has exploded. Somehow, when Lilli was captured, she was able to release that energy on an atomic level and use it as a means to kill Crane and escape. But as I said, the process is inevitably irreversible.

"By any estimate, she should be dead by now and so should we for that matter, with the level of radiation that she should be emitting, but she is able to neutralize it somehow. From what I can tell, she appears to be able to slow down the release of this energy, causing some sort of regression within the chain reaction—which is, in itself, extraordinary, but there are consequences. We're seeing them now. The human body is not designed to contain that amount of energy. She can't repair herself faster than the damage is done. And we don't have the capacity to stop it."

Hasaam trailed off as they heard the door to Lilli's room open behind them. Liam turned hopefully and watched as Joel stepped into the hallway and looked at him with red eyes set in a calm, smooth face. The resignation that Liam saw there enraged him.

"So, she's dying. Is that what you're trying to tell me?" Liam asked Hasaam coldly as he watched Joel close the door to the room where Alessandra was still working to put Lilli back together.

"Not in the sense that you mean," Joel answered quietly. "She is transcending from the physical world. She is becoming something more."

Liam stared back at Joel as if he was looking at the very cause of Lilli's death.

"I don't want to hear that shit right now," he spat. "If she can't be-"

"-That shit saved her life!" Joel snapped, getting right in Liam's face. "She did it to fight him. She *chose* this to protect you from having to find her so ripped apart you wouldn't recognize her. Would you have rather her suffer and die like that so that you could have a body to bury?"

Liam's face was frozen in defiance, but he couldn't help the shudder that passed down his spine or the tears that pricked his eyes at the very notion of someone hurting his sister that way.

Joel stepped back and looked away. The anguish Liam tried to hide was too raw for him to be around if he was going to keep his own despair at bay. Joel had wanted his words to be encouraging—the bright side of a horrible situation in which they were powerless to do anything. But his words were no match for their pain, and Liam tore right through them. They were both broken already, Joel realized. There was no need to make it worse.

"I know you think she won't be here, that she'll disappear into nothing, but it's not true," Joel finally said. "She will be everything."

Liam couldn't bring himself to say he was sorry, even though he truly was. He knew that Joel loved his sister—from the moment he saw them together he knew this. Up until he saw Joel's face in the hallway, Liam hadn't realized how much he had been counting on Joel to do what he always did—what no one else could do. He'd been suspending disbelief, waiting for Joel to come out of Lilli's room and tell him that what he saw was not real, that it meant something other than the obvious.

Around them, something had drawn the attention of the crowd, but they hardly noticed. Both men traded weary glances, finally too drained to fight each other.

Liam opened his mouth to apologize, but Joel raised his hand before he could speak.

"I know. I know you better than that; I shouldn't have reacted that way. You should go, see her before you leave," Joel said as he walked away.

Liam was about to ask what he meant when Jared rushed towards him with a small piece of paper in his hand.

"She's alive," Jared said excitedly. "There are reports from Afghanistan that say she's alive."

Liam stared back at Jared in confusion. "Who's alive?"

"The girl from Afghanistan, they say her name is Ghazal, the one from the reports about the demons. They are reporting several sightings of her in the area. They think she is alive."

Jared waited until he saw a flicker of understanding in Liam's eyes before he extended the folded piece of paper out to him and watched as Liam read the flight and contact information that had been scrawled out hastily. When Liam looked up, he was speechless, but his eyes were filled with an unmistakable spark of hope.

"If you can find her," Jared continued, "maybe there's a chance."

"Thank you," Liam said, grasping Jared's thin shoulder in gratitude before heading off towards his sister's room.

●●‥●●

Liam entered the room to the sound of Alessandra humming an unfamiliar lullaby as she sat in a chair and stroked Lilli's temple softly with the tips of her fingers. Though Alessandra's back was towards him, as he drew closer he could see Lilli clearly. Her eyes were closed and her expression was peaceful as she lay curled up on the bed. The saffron light of the lamp near her bedside gave her sunken cheeks a beautiful, soft glow. For an instant, Liam could almost imagine that none of this was happening, that the last 24 hours—the last 4 years—were all an impossible nightmare.

But when Alessandra finally turned to him, the smile she offered through her silent tears was so brave and sad, he knew everything he feared was true.

"Is she asleep?" He whispered in a voice so frail he barely recognized it. Alessandra's lips trembled slightly, but she did not answer.

"No," Lilli replied. Her voice was raspy, but determined as she shifted her body slightly towards Liam. "I'm just listening to my sister-in-law sing to me. She says she can't hold a tune, but I love her voice. It makes me feel like I'm brand new."

When Lilli finally opened her eyes to meet his, Liam could see the hazel of her left eye was covered in red.

Liam bit the inside of his cheek to calm himself. With Lilli turned towards him and the lamp only able to illuminate half of her features, he could finally see what Neva and Hasaam had been trying to tell him. His sister was gaunt and pale—sick like he'd never seen her before in his life. As a child, Lilli never got sick. Even as a baby, he remembered her tiny body being strong, with cheeks that were plump and glowing with life—until now.

"How…how are you feeling?" He managed to ask.

"Not as bad as I look, I'd say, judging by your expression." Her dry lips pressed together in a teasing smile that Liam had no hope of returning.

The sorrow he felt was overwhelming, but he fought it with everything he had. *Now I understand Joel's expression*, he thought. *It wasn't resignation, but realization of all that was at stake—how all their paths had led them to this horrible, empty place.*

"Joel said you chose this." It was all Liam could think to say—the only steady thing to stand on.

"I did," Lilli said calmly. "I didn't want to leave you. I never want to leave you, but I did."

"How long do we have?"

"As long as we need."

"But Hasaam said that staying here…it's killing you."

Lilli's indulgent smile made him feel like he was the younger sibling.

"I'm healing, Liam. The next time you see me, I won't look like this. I'll be better. I will hold on as long as I need to."

As Liam went to wipe the tear from his face, he remembered the piece of paper that was now crumbled in his hand.

"Jared found something. The girl in Afghanistan, they say she is alive. If she can do what you did, maybe she knows a way to fix this, to stop this from happening."

Lilli looked at him solemnly before answering.

"I can't see her, whether or not that's because she is blocking me or she's moved beyond my sight, I don't know."

"I'm going to find her. I have to try."

"I know you do, Liam. It's important that you go. There are answers you need to find there, I just don't know if they are the ones you're looking for."

Liam nodded as he tucked the piece of paper into his back pocket.

This is what I can do, he told himself, as he dried the last of his tears from his face with the palm of his hand.

"You don't know everything," Liam said earnestly as he sat carefully beside her at the foot of the bed, settling his left hand on Alessandra's thigh while he reached for Lilli's hand with his right.

"Sometimes, that's true," Lilli replied as her smile broadened. "Sometimes, that's true."

●•⋯•●

Katia followed Joel up the stairs from a distance. She'd never seen him like this. The man she'd come to know as so full of life, so much like his father, was a statue as he stared over the second-floor railing and looked down on the scene below. Though Katia knew he was aware of everything taking place around him—Liam and Jared's exchange, those gathered around the TV watching the latest massacre, and further off, Ngozi and Eli leading the detox effort with Michael, Nina, and Aaron. But his face betrayed none of this. Everything about him was lifeless and still except for the tears running down his face.

She stopped beside him, quietly giving him ample time to adjust to the intrusion into his private space before she spoke.

"I believe we will find a solution to this. There has to be another way," she said fervently while keeping her eyes on the crowd below.

"I hope you are right," Joel replied, but there was no trace of hope in his voice.

"Lilli is strong, as strong as you are. She will make it through."

"You forget how many times I've done this," Joel answered. "My father, my mother, and now, my wife. You'd think I'd be used to losing everything I love by now."

"You don't know that," Katia insisted, hoping that it was true. "And this isn't like Marcus…"

"No, it isn't, but it feels exactly the same."

At first, Katia didn't know what to say. Their abilities didn't make them immune to suffering, and Joel had suffered more than most. She knew firsthand exactly how consuming that kind of pain could be, how, after a while, all suffering began to feel the same, no matter the cause.

Marcus' death had left its mark on all of them, but she was finally healing from it. For the first time in her life, she felt a deep hope growing inside her, growing out of nothing more than the certainty that she was finally exactly who and where she was meant to be.

"No, I don't believe that. I refuse. It can't end this way. If I'm still alive, if you're still alive, if *she's* still alive, then there must be something we can do."

The conviction in her voice pulled his attention away from his own sadness. She was scared, just as they all were, but her thoughts weren't held captive by her fear. Instead she was searching—fighting—to see past the blind spots that the demons created in her vision to get to the place where they could make a difference and win.

He hadn't realized how much Katia had changed until this moment.

Joel took a deep breath as he watched the flurry of activity below. Everywhere he looked, people were moving with purpose and determination. Whether it was phone calls to the Seer Rescue Centers to organize resources and logistics or the large Quorum that was taking place to transfer information and coordinate blocking efforts throughout the Collective or giving needed medical attention to those in need, what they planned to do—what they were *destined* to do—was already in motion. They were all just waiting for Lilli and Joel to recover from their wounds, rejoin the whole, and assume their roles in bringing about the things to come.

Lead them, Joel told himself. *This is why you're not in the bed right next to her. You have to lead...like he did.*

Joel clung to the memory of his father as he forced himself to stand up straight and face Katia.

"You're right. This is not the end. Not even close. Tell everybody to meet me in the conference room in five minutes. I know what we need to do next."

CHAPTER 12: THE PLAN

Four minutes after Joel had given the charge, the conference room was packed with conference calls and video links with every Rescue Center in their operation. Joel stood at the front of the large space, speaking in a voice that was both gentle and commanding, as only he could.

"As always seems to be the case with us, we don't have much time, so I'll keep this brief. Anyone who is going to go by plane needs to be in the air and out of here within the next 2 hours, so let's get started. As everyone here knows by now, the Guild will not help us in our efforts to defeat the demons who are hunting us. In fact, we suspect that at least one of the leaders within the Guild has made a secret alliance with them to capture and kill every single one of us, regardless of how many innocent lives are lost in the bargain. We will need every Seer we have in the Collective to do what we can for the people who need our help the most.

"I know that it will be hard to do the things we are about to do—to be hunted by the same people we are trying to save. But remember, we are the only ones who can fight this battle. We are the only ones who can defeat these demons who prey on the innocent to get to us. The fact that we can do it, that we have been given these abilities, means that we were *meant* to do it. And if we can endure this, no matter what the cost to each of us, we will give this world a chance to reclaim itself once more—and that is what we have been fighting for all along."

"So...besides imminent death, what's the plan?" Vincent called out from the crowd.

Joel smiled.

"Maura and Tenzen, we need you to work with Alma to coordinate tracking of the demons' movements so that we can try to be in a position to protect as many people as possible. Alma will explain to you the full extent of our network and resources and how they can be used. Alma will also help you train others on how to fight these creatures. Your experience in Geneva will help prepare others for what to expect. Use Quorums and the Collective to train as many of us as you can, then move out. I will do the same from here.

"These demons won't hesitate to use innocent people to draw us out, so don't be taken by surprise. Once the Guild has made their move, we will need to mobilize quickly. Our first line of defense should always be to draw the demons away from populated areas, but this will be difficult. They are used to hiding in plain sight, so if that fails, our goal is to hold them off for as long as possible to give those in danger a chance to escape."

Joel's face conveyed very little of the conflict he felt inside as he looked into the faces of those who were trusting him with their lives.

"The truth is, there aren't enough of us to fight them all-"

Joel was interrupted as Emma stood up with her newly shorn head and raised her voice above the murmur of the group.

"I speak for all of us who you rescued from the Guild in Chicago the day your father died when I tell you that we are ready to fight." When she was finished, Mai, Ammon, and Sonja stood up with her. Each of them had shaved off the last remnant of their lives with the Guild. Their eyes blazed with the knowledge of new powers that they couldn't wait to test.

Joel smiled at them as he motioned for them to sit down.

"Thank you, Emma. Tess has told me that you are ready and if you're willing, you will go wherever you are needed, just as I will. Our numbers can't be helped, but I believe we can be smarter than they are and work together to do what we can."

"But what about Lilli?" Tess asked anxiously.

"After the plan is in place, I will join Maura and Tenzen wherever I'm needed. Lilli will join when she is able, but given her condition, we will need to be cautious about how and when we use her abilities. We're still trying to figure it out. We don't know what's safe for her at this point." Joel wanted to say more, but he couldn't let his focus drift into worry, at least not until he was done. He cleared his throat and continued.

"In the meantime, Alessandra and Liam will head to Afghanistan to investigate the reports that the girl who killed one of the demons is still alive. If there's a chance that we can learn more about how to defeat these things and stay alive, then we need to get that information."

Joel paused for a moment to make sure each Seer in the room had the chance to absorb the severity of what he was asking of them and waited until he was certain they understood.

"How can we help, Joel?" Eli asked anxiously.

"We need three things," Joel replied without hesitation. "First, as you know, Ngozi was able to get some blood and tissue samples from one of the demons off Vincent's clothes. She has begun to run some tests, but we need a full analysis of what we are dealing with. Any understanding of how they camouflage themselves as human or potential weaknesses could be invaluable to us. Your assistance with this would be appreciated.

"But we also need someone to take a fresh look at why they are attacking the locations they've chosen. The news reports say they are random attacks, but I don't believe that. The creatures I fought were focused, cunning, thoughtful. Their actions were not random, and we can't afford to underestimate them. Lilli can sense their presence, but that is not enough—we need to know where they'll be before they get there. If we can figure out what they are after, then we can do more than just minimize the damage they cause. If we know why they are doing what they are doing, we might be able to stop them.

"And last, we need you to begin work on a better detox serum than the one we have, one that can accelerate the recovery process while minimizing the side effects."

"Why?" Eli asked. "The one we have worked perfectly on Emma and the others."

"Yes, but it requires months of recovery that we don't have anymore. We're going to need every Seer the Guild has if we are going to win this fight. When the time comes, we'll need them to be ready."

With a final nod from Joel, the room cleared out almost as quickly as it filled, slowly revealing a frail woman who leaned heavily against the doorframe, smiling proudly at him.

She was far from healed, with her hair damp and matted against her thin face, but the sight of Lilli standing on her own two feet again filled his entire body with a hope only she could give him. He smiled broadly back at her.

Andreas was a crazed man as he stood before the surviving members of the Guild, pleading for them to take their last chance at survival. Bloody from his injuries and the roughing-up that Saubos had given him after he was dragged away from the scene that the Lost Seers had escaped, Andreas shook with the knowledge that convincing the men and women before him to agree with his plan was his last chance to stay alive.

Though he couldn't tell them, his mandate was clear—use the Guild resources to root out the Lost Seers or die. *Each and every one of you,*

Saubos had promised, refusing to take his human form until Andreas agreed. He knew Saubos was waiting just outside the door, observing the meeting as it took place. If he couldn't make this work, he and the five others in the room with him would die right where they stood.

"Listen to me. This is the only way we can proceed. It's a gamble. But we're not gambling anything we're not already about to lose. Think about it. All we have to do is tell the truth. You saw it yourself today. They don't want us. They want the Seers. All we have to do is issue a call for all the Lost Seers to turn themselves in and let the public know that if they refuse, all of us will be annihilated in the process. We can ask them to help us save humanity by giving up the people who are already abominations in our society. We can use the fear we have created about the Seers to our advantage—to save ourselves."

"Why would we turn over the one group of people able to fight them. That's suicide," Deidra countered.

"Because there aren't enough of them to ensure victory," Yusef answered.

"We could help them, fight with them. What about the girl in Afghanistan? They say she may still be alive. We could try to find her, find out what she knows," Deidra countered while watching Andreas carefully.

"We can't count on rumors." Andreas replied. "That girl may have killed one of them, but she most likely killed herself in the process. Did you see what happened to Lilli, the Seer who saved you? It looked like the process of killing that demon almost killed her.

"Besides, how many of Joel's Seers do you think there are?" Andreas continued. "Even if they had hundreds at their disposal, how many of them can stand up against what we saw today? Maybe a handful at best. Those that were here today barely escaped with their lives. How can they save us when they can't even save themselves?"

"And what makes you think they will spare us, when all of this is over and we've handed our only defense to the enemy?"

"Nothing is certain, Deidra, except the fact that if we do not yield to these creatures, we will die. The solution I'm proposing will at least buy us time to learn our enemy while minimizing the loss of life for billions of innocent people. We will deal with these creatures once we have contained the threat, but for now, our first duty is survival."

Deidra sat back in her chair silently as the others agreed.

"How would we implement this strategy?" Yusef asked.

"We hold a press conference, telling them what happened today. I don't think the Seers under our control are a threat; otherwise, they would have pursued them when Joel's group left. I think they are after them because they pose a threat to their survival, small though it may be. Ironically, this gives us a common enemy with these creatures and a situation I believe we can still use to our advantage.

"Once we identify the Lost Seers as the cause of these attacks, people will clamor to turn them over just to survive. We should be able to sit back and let things play out on their own. If the demons win, they will have eliminated the problem of the Lost Seers and gotten the public to round up Seers for us to replenish our ranks.

And on the off chance that the Seers prove strong enough to defeat them, then we simply congratulate the few that will remain on a job well done. Either way, we survive."

The room was silent, filled with a quiet desperation that Andreas hoped would tip things in his favor.

"Get it done, Andreas, and thank you for your leadership in this," Yusef said finally as the most senior member of the Guild.

"You have my word," Andreas said quietly. His hand trembled as he opened the door to the small meeting room and stepped into the empty hall.

Flashing lights blinded him as he stood before the press corps members who were brave enough to assemble in front of what was left of the Guild's headquarters structure. They had been shown video footage of the damage inside and were clamoring with questions and fear. As Andreas stepped to the podium, he imagined them as hungry animals just waiting to be thrown the next fat piece of meat.

He hadn't bothered to wash or change, leaving his ripped clothes, blood, and bruises on display as he spoke wearily into the microphone.

"I know you all have many questions for me today, but I implore you to hold them until the end. I come to you as a representative of the UWO and the Guild with an urgent message that we believe will save lives as we deal with the devastating plague that has ravaged our cities and homes.

"Twelve hours ago, we held a meeting with Joel Akida and his cohorts in an attempt to put aside our difference and use their unique abilities to address the global crisis before us. During that meeting, we were attacked by five of the very demons that we have seen all over the world. While many were killed in the battle that followed, one thing became unavoidably clear as we tried to survive this awful ordeal: the demons that attacked us were not after the Guild members or our staff. With each and every one of their actions, it became clear that what they were truly after were the members of the Lost Seers.

"While we don't yet know the reason for their interest in this group, it is imperative that we move quickly to minimize the loss of life for our citizens around the world. Therefore, we are calling on each member of the Lost Seers, wherever you are around the world, to turn themselves in to be quarantined from the rest of the population.

"To all others, for your own safety and for the survival of the human race, we urge you to remove yourself from anyone you know to be a Seer or who confesses to be a Seer. Please encourage these individuals to turn themselves in voluntarily. If they refuse, please contact your local authorities so that they may be removed from the general population to reduce loss of life. I repeat, any Seer who is not quarantined with us presents an imminent threat to the survival of our society and must surrender or be handed over to proper authorities immediately. As a precaution, we will be ceasing all travel by air and monitoring all other modes of transportation vigorously until further notice. We realize that these measures will present significant inconveniences to our citizens, but we ask you to consider what is at stake if we do not act quickly to contain this threat. We will update you on any new strategies we have to alleviate this crisis as they are developed."

Andreas knew that his statement was being televised worldwide, and as he looked over the crowd of reporters jostling for his attention, he could almost see his words spread like wildfire in a forest, sparking the kindling nearby, then fanning out to the low bushes and shrubs until it reached the tall trees. From there the fire would be seen for miles, burning anything that opposed it and purifying the land to start anew.

"When does the quarantine start?" He heard one reporter shout over the crowd. Andreas turned to Saubos, who stood conspicuously at the edge of the crowd. Saubos met Andreas' glance and nodded approvingly. Andreas contained his excitement and relief as he returned his attention to the reporter who asked the question he had been waiting to answer.

"The quarantine begins now."

Chapter 13: The Purge

Things had been bad before, but nothing like this. In the weeks that followed the Guild's announcement, the manhunt to identify and round up every Lost Seer in every corner of the world was unleashed. In addition to the ruthlessness with which the Guild had always pursued the Lost Seers, what set this time apart from any other since the Guild began its first gathering was the almost zealous extent to which average citizens participated in the search for and capture of Seers.

What began as a call for the quarantine of all Lost Seers quickly turned into a hunt of anyone suspected of knowing or being a Seer. Makeshift enforcement groups began to form as a means of cleansing their neighborhood of any elements that might draw the attention of the demons that continued to terrorize communities everywhere. Paranoia gave way to brutality as innocent people, most of whom were not Seers, were dragged out into the street and beaten by their neighbors before being turned over to local authorities. Eventually, orders to merely identify Seers for quarantine were ignored as people took matters into their own hands, deciding to exterminate what they saw as the cause of all the chaos around them. Even with the sweeping resources of the Guild, it didn't take long before most of the violence against Seers and non-Seers alike was perpetrated by civilians, who, in their desperation to stay alive, lost all sense of the humanity that makes life valuable.

In public, the Guild discouraged these vigilante groups, urging restraint in identifying and reporting suspected Seers. On the ground, it was a different story. Local Guild units used the resurgence in fear of the Seers to stamp out the sympathy that had been growing in the past few months as a result of Nadia Spencer's interviews with Joel Akida and Ming Jhu. Though the Guild risked losing valuable Seers, they reasoned that it was more advantageous to use the vigilante groups to help them reestablish their control over the Seers by closing off any pockets where they might hide and refortify their resistance.

But as horrific as the unfolding events were, they were not worse than what Joel and those within the Collective had foreseen. After eight years of preparation, they were ready.

It began with Adaline Renoit's recovery. Watching her heal from an illness that Joel's gift had identified helped him recognize the value in his abilities for the first time. From that moment on, Joel committed himself to learning how to use his gift to make a difference. Slowly, as Joel realized the full extent of his power, he began seeking out the people and resources he would need to build a network of safe havens where other Seers could develop their skills in freedom, as he did. With

Xavier's help, it took him almost 8 years to build the forty-seven Seer Rescue Centers that now existed across the world—all stocked and ready for the events to come.

In heavily populated cities like Paris, most Rescue Centers looked like little more than rundown row houses from the outside. But in rural areas, like the center Alma ran in Cuba, Joel was able to build state-of-the-art underground facilities hidden among farms so as not to raise local suspicions.

Each facility was administered by a Seer whom Joel had personally recruited and could trust implicitly with the responsibility of guiding other Seers towards the fulfillment of their gifts. Just as he had drawn Maura, Katia, and others to the Commune in Iowa, Joel had used his ability to draw other Seers to the Rescue Centers.

But as with so many things, the vision of the battle they would need to fight barely prepared them for the experience of fighting three enemies at once. The clarity of sight and blocking required to evade the Guild's relentless pursuit alone could have easily debilitated them if they were not prepared. Between the Guild's soldiers and the growing crop of vigilantes who took it upon themselves to determine which of its citizens were and were not a threat, the Seers' efforts to protect the innocent were challenged on every side. The blind spots caused by the demons only made things infinitely more dangerous.

Though Lilli could predict their general presence, she could not pinpoint their exact locations during an event without tipping the balance that would endanger her life. And so the Seers fought through the blind spots as best they could. Most times they escaped, managing to fight and evade the Guild or the demons to bring Seers and other innocent people to safety. But other times, their best was not enough to save them.

At the start of the Guild's quarantine campaign, there were just under 2,000 Seers in the Collective. While each of them had honed their abilities beyond the extraordinary, they were still vulnerable to all the things that made them human. As valiantly as they fought, there simply weren't enough of them to match the efforts of their enemies. In the hours before the Guild had announced their campaign, Seers throughout the Collective had moved swiftly to get ahead of the tide that was coming for them, knowing that the impending global shut down of all airports would make traveling to the places they were needed slow and more dangerous than ever. In the worst of the fighting, at least one Seer died for every village they saved.

And though it was hard to deal with the loss of their presence within the Collective that bound them together, their grief only made everyone around them more determined to push forward no matter what.

It took Liam and Alessandra two weeks to get to the caves where Ghazal first disappeared. It was precious time they hated to lose, but there was nothing they could do. At first they had planned to take their chartered plane directly into Afghanistan, masquerading as reporters from the US press corps, but the Guild's air flight surveillance forced them to land five and a half hours into their eight hour flight in Azerbaijan. From there they took a ferry across the Caspian Sea to Turkmenistan where they met Jalo, a trusted associate of Joel's smuggler who promised to take them into Afghanistan as part of a UWO supplies convoy for a mere $50,000 cash. Even though the night was too dark to see the water that was lapping at the boat behind them, Liam could still make out Jalo's gold teeth shining underneath his grin as he took the money Alessandra paid him. They changed into some traditional clothing that Jalo had bought for them while he counted his money in silence. Liam kept his hand on his gun most of the night, even though Alessandra had already told him that it wouldn't be necessary.

With the exception of a few bandits who tried to rob the convoy for food, they made it across Turkmenistan without incident. To Liam's surprise, Jalo had been the one to make sure the bandits escaped alive with a bit of food to carry home when the UWO staff had wanted to shoot to kill.

"Hunger is not a crime," Jalo barked as he yanked a gun out of one of the UWO serviceman's hands. "And besides, killing is bad for my business. I get paid to deliver supplies, not bodies."

"Do the bandits come because of the quarantine?" Alessandra asked quietly when they had a moment alone while the trucks refueled.

"Out here things were always hard, but now, with no planes to carry food, the wait is too long for some. Soon they will come from as far as Uzbekistan, my country, just for food."

Jalo dropped them off just outside Kabul where he had arranged to have a car waiting for them, packed with supplies, a satellite phone and a map to a labyrinth of caves where Ghazal was said to be hiding. Liam didn't realize how much he would miss Jalo until he watched him disappear in a cloud of dust as he drove away.

Considering that they had been riding in the back of a truck for days, the hour long drive to Bamiyan felt almost invigorating until they arrived. The valley below the cliffs had been covered with reporters and people that Alessandra identified from her sight as spies for the Guild. They slept that night on the side of the mountain until the first light of day allowed them to find the opening to the caves.

Prepared to spend the next few days wandering though the inside of the mountain, Liam and Alessandra took their time. They traveled down each opening until they found the first of several families hiding from the press and the demons, they swore they could hear rattling in the walls of their caves every night. Liam relied on his Farsi to English dictionary while Alessandra used her connection with those within the Collective who spoke Farsi to ask and translate questions. Slowly they learned that the people in the caves had not heard any rumors about Ghazal's whereabouts and that no one had seen her alive since she had jumped weeks ago.

With each day they travelled up the mountain through the inner network of caves, Liam grew more and more quiet, letting Alessandra do the talking for them as he became lost in his own thoughts. By the seventh day, they had reached the upper-most level of caves, where they could actually feel the breeze rushing in from the outside. It was a welcome change from the stagnant air that had been turning their stomachs for the past week. They settled for the night at the base of what the families inside the cave had begun to call The Forbidden Place—the mouth of the cave where Ghazal was last seen. It was dark outside, dark enough to go unnoticed as Liam looked out from the cliff onto the charred remains of the village below.

Despite how high up they were, the night was hot enough that they didn't need a fire, but Liam still shivered in the blanket of warm air around him. Absently, he traced a small drawing etched into the wall as he stared out into the dark. The emptiness inside felt as vast as the landscape before him, and he had to look away before the grief pulled him over.

This is the last thing she saw before she fell, he thought. Tired of fighting it, Liam closed his eyes and finally admitted out loud what he had been thinking for days.

"We're not going to find her, are we?"

His words were more of an admission to the sky and the stars than a question to anyone else. Besides him and Alessandra, there was no one around, which was exactly why they had chosen this spot to rest for the night before their descent in the morning.

Behind him, Alessandra had laid down against the cave wall watching him.

"I don't know, Liam. We have looked for her, all of us. If she is alive, her power has moved beyond our abilities to recognize."

"Which means she's dead."

Alessandra knew he wouldn't turn around until she told him the truth. She was so tired, it felt like it took all her strength to simply lift her body up from the soft sleeping bag Liam had prepared for her and answer him.

"Yes, I think so," she said before lowering herself back down to the ground.

Liam took a moment to breathe the truth in. By the time he turned around, Alessandra was snoring softly. Surprised, Liam looked at her for what felt like the first time in days. The bread and olives that he laid out for her were uneaten. Her canteen was half full. Something was off, but he couldn't figure out what. They had been walking and climbing all day for seven days, but her appetite only seemed to get worse with each passing day. When he'd mentioned it two days ago, she'd said it was the smell of the caves, but now he wasn't so sure. The air around them now was clean, warm.

She should be starving, he thought. He knew the climb was steep and dangerous at times, but it was nothing she shouldn't have been able to handle.

Over the past few days, they had been working so hard to find Ghazal that they'd had little time to themselves, and when they did, he'd found it hard to keep the dread of what it would mean if they didn't find Ghazal from his thoughts. Between the lack of privacy and his dwindling morale, they hadn't had a chance to really connect in days.

He knelt down beside her and touched her forehead with only the slightest tremble in his hands.

Besides a first aid kit, they had no real medical supplies. As his hand trailed over the skin on her head and neck, he tried to recall anything she could have eaten that would have made her ill. Though many of the families had graciously shared their water from the underground well inside the mountain, they had been careful to add the purification drops that were designed to kill anything that could have made them sick.

She doesn't have a fever, he noted with some relief, *but her hands are never this cold.*

Liam could feel the panic growing as he rubbed his hands roughly against his jeans, trying to resist the urge to wake her up and ask if she was feeling ok.

She just needs to rest, he told himself as he leaned over to place two fingers on the pulse at her neck.

To his surprise, Alessandra's heart was pounding even though her face looked peaceful and still. Her eyes flew open before he could count to ten.

"I'm sorry I woke you," he started to say before she jolted upright.

"They're coming! They're already here!" She gasped.

And then they heard it, the sound of something hard and terrible crashing into the side of the mountain.

CHAPTER 14: THE SIGN

The impact shook their bodies like a hammer, rattling the very bones underneath their skin. Stones and dust shook free from the walls around them as the creatures outside crashed into the mountain.

Liam barely had time to reach for Alessandra's hand and pull her to her feet before another crash rocked them back into the wall, unable to move, unable to escape.

They held hands tightly while their eyes were fixed on the large chunks of earth that were falling away from the mouth of the cave, exposing them to the outside where they would be defenseless.

"No!" Liam heard Alessandra scream as her body pitched forward, towards the edge of the cave that had grown from a six to ten foot opening in a matter of seconds.

Liam tried to pull her back, but lost his footing as the ground rumbled underneath them. From the cave's opening he could see that there were two beasts outside, working in some insane tandem effort to bring down the mountain and them along with it. He made another attempt to steady himself enough to pull her back, but the impact of another blow forced his body sideways. Her fingers slipped free from his. Liam's hands hit the ground to brace his fall and found the ground cracking in two beneath them. He sprang up quickly only to find himself on the wrong side of the divide, with the sand slipping out from underneath his feet as the gap widened.

For the first time in his life, Liam felt like he could actually see the future. Everything around him seemed to synchronize with the slow pounding of blood in his head. In front of him, Alessandra stood at the other side of the gaping fissure between them. Her back was turned away from him so that she could face the beasts that could now see her clearly from where she stood near the mouth of the cave.

Even while staring death in the face, Liam thought she looked strangely unhurried and serene with her loose linen clothes and long hair rippling in the turbulence of the air. He imagined that Alessandra was standing exactly where Ghazal had stood and that they were seeing exactly what Ghazal had seen the night she died.

Just as we are about to die, he thought.

In a quiet space of his mind, he marveled at the irony of having come to solve the mystery of Ghazal's death only to have the answer revealed through suffering the same fate. In the calm between dreams and nightmares, he watched Alessandra stretch out her arm. There was a blue glow of light within her hand that Liam was sure he'd seen only once before.

The winged beast before her sneered and snapped as his body hovered well outside of her reach.

"You will not hurt him," Liam heard her say as the light took form in her hands.

"No! No!" Liam shouted as he reached out for her, only to be forced back by the ground dissolving underneath his feet. The gap between them had become a chasm, swallowing up the ground. Backed up to the wall, Liam couldn't get a running start to cross the hole that was now at least ten feet wide and growing rapidly.

"Alessandra, don't! Don't!" Liam heard himself say, even though he wasn't sure what he was asking of her. He just knew he couldn't lose her. Hearing the despair in his voice, Alessandra turned back to look at him. There was only peace on her face as she whispered, "Don't be afraid."

"Behind you!" Liam shouted as his eyes shifted from the calm on her face to the demon who was darting forward, trying to take advantage of her momentary distraction. But before he could reach her, Alessandra's head snapped back, holding him frozen in place. Then the dirt under her feet gave way.

For an instant, Liam was suspended in a perfect moment of horror and disbelief as he watched the ground beneath her open up and pull her under.

She fell.

She fell.

And then he jumped down after her.

●•··•●

The sound of trickling water was faint but welcoming. Even better—she could taste the moisture, the freshness on her tongue. She took her breaths in slowly, assessing with every intake, while focusing her pain outward, as she needed.

Be careful, she told herself. *You need to reserve your energy.*

Beside her, Liam lay peacefully against the jagged rock that had split his skull. But there would be no scar where it punctured his temple, no trace of the damage to his frontal lobe or the fracture to his femur. His body simply needed a chance to burn off the last of the adrenaline and rest. And while she could restore him completely, the drain to her own energy reserves was too high. So she let his body do the rest, knowing he would wake up soon.

The underground water cave was wide and hollow around them, one of the many that were rumored to exist inside these mountains. They were notoriously hard to find. Alessandra could only thank God that this one had found them. With the exception of the rocks that had fallen in with them, the ground beneath them was soft, smooth dirt, and Alessandra was grateful for the small comfort it gave them both.

Without a shred of light to define even a small outline of their surroundings, Alessandra waited in the dark, listening to the water and the sound of Liam's breathing. When he did finally wake with a start, her name was the first word out of his mouth.

"Alessandra?" His voice was rich and deep. She smiled.

"I'm here, Liam."

"Keep talking... I can't see you. Are you hurt?"

She could hear him moving slowly across the ground, taking the same path she had taken hours ago.

"I'm only a few feet away."

When he reached her, the warmth of his hand still took her by surprise.

"Are you alright?" Liam whispered as he traced her forehead with his fingertips.

"Yes, I'm fine."

But the fact that she had not moved towards him in anyway let him know that she was not. Ignoring her, Liam continued his assessment, trailing over her arms and the sides of her torso for any signs of pain.

"Are you trying to get some?" She teased, hoping to distract him, but he didn't bite. Alessandra let him get as far as the torn fabric of her pants leg before she caught his hand.

"Liam, I'm fine. Please," she tried again, but there was tension in her voice.

"Where?" His touch was gentler now, more furtive, as he continued down her leg.

"It's nothing, just my ankle. Just a sprain."

Alessandra could close her eyes and almost see the scowl that must have been on his face.

"Can you move it at all?"

"Yes, but I'd rather not."

He was about to ask which one until he felt her right ankle, which was several millimeters larger than her left. She let out a low, measured breath as he lifted her calf to elevate it. The next thing she heard was the ripping of fabric as he tore his shirt to bandage her ankle.

"Is there anywhere else?" He asked, letting his worry seep through his voice. "Please tell me the truth. I can't see your face."

"I'm fine, Liam. It just needs time to heal on its own. I promise, nothing else is wrong with me."

She could hear his sigh of relief as he kissed the swollen arch of her foot.

They were silent for a long time, just staring at each other through the dark until he finally spoke.

"I love you," he said softly as he cradled her leg on his lap. "I thought before you fell... I thought you were going to do what Lilli did."

"I know what you thought. I heard it in your voice. I saw it on your face, and I don't ever want you to think that. I can't make that choice. Not now, not ever. I have everything to live for. *We* have everything to live for."

"I just...I don't know what's happening. I don't know how to fix what's happening. I can't even see to get us out of, wherever the hell we are."

"You can't change what will happen, Liam. That's not why we're here. But I know we will survive this, Liam. I don't know how, but I know we will."

Liam nodded his head even though she couldn't see him. The feeling of helplessness threatened to consume him again, but, as always, he found the strength to beat it back.

As long as we're alive, there's hope, he told himself. *As long as we're alive, we can find a way.*

And that's when he heard the sound of water trickling in.

"This could be one of the underground caves where people get their water. If I'm right, then there's gotta be a tunnel leading out of here. I'm going to look around. If I can find a tunnel, maybe we can crawl through, see if any of the families here survived, and make our way down the mountain."

"Liam, I'm not sure how well I can move right now."

"Don't worry. I can carry you if I need to. We'll make it work," he answered while placing her leg down on a rock that was covered with something soft.

"What is that?" She asked, trying to move slightly to get a better sense of the fabric. She regretted it instantly.

"Stay still. It's just my jacket."

"Be careful," she warned. "It's not warm down here. You should put it back on."

"I'm good for now." From the sound of his voice, she could already tell that he was a good distance away from her. "I'm just trying to find the wall…"

Liam's voice trailed off as he crawled around in the dark. He kept his body low, extending one hand out in front of him and another above his head just in case the ceiling was low.

Once he found it, Liam felt around the wall for several moments before he came to a series of large rocks that were stuck within a large crevice. "Okay. I think I found it," Liam announced as he rose safely to his knees.

"I can feel the entrance, but it's blocked. It may have collapsed during the attack, but I can't tell for sure. I'm going to try to clear it, but it's going to take me awhile.

He worked carefully for over an hour before Alessandra interrupted him.

"Liam, stop! Do you feel that?"

Liam let a large boulder roll from his hand before becoming completely still. He'd been so consumed with his work and the emptiness of the dark that he hadn't heard anything but the piling of rocks around him.

"What is it?" He asked.

"I don't know. Just listen."

For what seemed like an eternity in the dark, he couldn't hear or feel anything, but just as he was about to ask again, he felt it—the slightest tremor beneath his feet. It was so faint, he was almost sure he imagined it before he heard a loud but muffled voice just beyond their cave.

"عجله کردن" Hurry Up!

"بسرعت" Quickly!

There were more muffled voices— – then silence.

"Liam…" Alessandra whispered before her voice was overrun by the sound of a jackhammer grinding just outside the entrance Liam had been trying to clear. The vibration of the jackhammer shook the walls around them, sending small rocks and dust raining down from the ceiling above.

Liam retraced his steps immediately, ignoring the small scrapes to his hands as he made his way back down the path that led to Alessandra. His only intention had been to shield her from the raining debris, but when he got to where he felt sure he'd left her, she was gone. Fear made him feel like the temperature in the cave had dropped fifty degrees in a heartbeat, then he felt something brush the side of his leg. In the dark, with no way of knowing who or what it was, he almost screamed.

"Liam, I'm here," Alessandra shouted over the jackhammer. "Against the wall. I'm alright. Come."

Slowly, he felt his way. When he finally reached her, he wedged his body between hers and the wall as best he could and drew his knife from his back pocket.

The chill he'd fought against a moment ago was gone. His body was covered with sweat.

We're trapped, he thought. *There's no way out of here.*

He felt the tension in Alessandra's arms as they wrapped around his back. He turned towards the sensation of her breath right below his ear. And without seeing anything, he knew she was right there with him—eyes wide open in the dark, looking towards the sound of the jackhammer.

"Can you see anything?" He asked just loud enough for her to hear him over the deafening noise.

"Not clearly, which means the demons must be close by or involved somehow. I see five men, but I don't know who they are."

Suddenly the pounding of the jackhammer stopped and was quickly replaced by the sound of metal scraping and moving the debris away. From what Liam could tell, they had managed to move more rocks in three minutes than he'd done in an hour. Then the voice came again, clearer and closer than before.

"عجله کردن" *Hurry Up!*

"بسرعت" *Quickly!*

Liam thought that it was the same voice, but he couldn't be sure. One more blast of the jackhammer and they could be through.

"I'm going to head over to the entrance. See if I can catch the first one who enters," Liam whispered directly into her ear.

"Yes," Alessandra agreed. "I'll take the rest."

Liam had to smile at that.

"The ceiling is pretty high at this point. I'll help you stand."

"No," she whispered back, "I'll manage on my own, when I'm ready."

There was no arguing. At this point, they needed to trust each other if they were going to make it out alive. By the time Liam kissed the palm of her hand and got to his feet, the hammering had begun again. Though it took more time than Liam had expected, it was still sooner than he'd hoped.

Their only advantage was the sliver of light that streamed in behind the first figure who entered the cave.

CHAPTER 15: THE BRIDGE

Liam caught him by the throat and drew him in, knocking the gun from his hand easily.

"به من کمک کنید!" *Please help me!* The man cried out before Liam pressed his knife to the hollow skin underneath his jaw. He gagged and tugged, but could not escape Liam's grasp.

With the light coming in from the opening, Liam's eyes could finally see the outline of their cave. He checked to see if Alessandra was standing but found an empty space where she had been. But he didn't have time to seek her out before four other men rushed through the tunnel and into the cave. At first they couldn't see anything with Liam behind them, pressed back into the shadow of the wall.

"Fardeen! Fardeen!" They shouted into the dark as their eyes tried to adjust. By then, Fardeen had given up fighting against Liam and stood still and helpless as his friends wandered into Alessandra's trap.

"ما باید به اینجا می آیند نمی کرده اند." *We should not have come here,* one of the men whispered before his body was suddenly pulled forward into the cave wall as if being grabbed and bound by some unseen hand. He screamed as one-by-one he watched his friends succumb to the darkness of the cave.

When they had all disappeared, only then did Alessandra step into the shaft of light that streamed in. The look on her face was hard and fierce, like he'd never seen her look before. If she was in pain from her ankle, there was no visible trace of it. Her stance was tall and powerful. Like all the other men surrounding her, he found himself staring at a stranger, and wondering who this woman was and what she would do next.

"Liam, send him to me," she commanded as she kept her eyes fixed on the four men frozen on the wall. As soon as Liam loosened his grip, he felt Fardeen being pulled from his hand to land face down on the ground in front of Alessandra.

"Why are you looking for us? What do you want?" Alessandra asked sharply.

In a panic the man answered in Farsi, rushing and stumbling through his words before Alessandra raised her hand and cut him off.

"I don't speak Farsi. I heard you speaking English outside the cave. Speak it now."

The man rose to his knees then and began unwrapping the turban from his head to reveal a symbol tattooed into the crest of his shaven head.

All the sternness drained from Alessandra's face as she stepped forward to get a closer look at what he was trying to show her. As she began to understand, tears sprang to her eyes. She looked at the four men she had bound against the wall and released them immediately. She had seen the symbol before in a vision Alma had shared with the Collective, but with no context she had not understood its meaning before now.

"ش.خبب ارم." *Forgive me*, she stammered in what little Farsi she could remember from her week-long trip through the mountain.

"I did not know," she continued softly to the man still kneeling before her. He met her gaze and nodded in understanding.

"What is it?" Liam asked, closing the distance between them.

"We are here to help you," the man said slowly as he traced the symbol on his scalp. "We are here to help Seers."

● ● · · ● ●

The plan was to follow the Khyber Pass into Pakistan, but with the roads so heavily guarded, they would have to travel on foot. Without a car, the journey was slow and difficult—especially for Alessandra who had to be carried most of the way. The show of strength that she displayed in the cave evaporated almost as quickly as it came once she realized they were safe.

As the only member of the group who spoke English, Fardeen helped Liam carry Alessandra on a makeshift stretcher while he shared the story of how he came to find them.

"At first, we assumed, like the demons obviously did, that you were dead. But then when we saw that a few families from inside the mountain had escaped, we decided to look for you. We'd almost given up, but then we heard you moving the rocks as we were leaving."

"Why were you looking for us in the first place?" Liam asked.

"Ghazal was my first cousin, but we grew up like brother and sister. She used to draw this symbol all the time, since she was a little girl. Her father taught us how to read and write. As children we practiced together. She would draw pictures and sign them with the symbol. Because I was older, I thought she did this because she hadn't yet learned how to write her name. When I tried to show her, she would push me away. She told me the drawing was not her name. It was who she was. As she grew older, whenever she would send me a letter, she would sign it this way. At the time, I didn't think about it. She was always strange, different.

"I hadn't seen her in many years because I was away at university. I was coming back for her wedding in a few months before everything happened. But I didn't make the connection until I saw my great aunt on the news comforting her mother. When she said Ghazal was a Seer, that's when I understood.

"I didn't get to say goodbye. Sometimes I can't help but wonder if I had understood earlier, maybe I could have done something to save her…" Fardeen's voice trailed off as he tried to shake off the emotion.

"I saw the symbol carved into the cave yesterday," Liam offered gently. "Did you put it there?"

"No. Ghazal must have. Sometime before her death. No one else knew about the symbol but us until I began to share it."

"What do you mean? I've never seen that symbol before yesterday."

"No, you wouldn't have. After her death, I just drew the symbol I had seen so many times and posted it on my Twitter account with the words, "She lives." I don't know why I said it that way. I was just grieving, I guess. But suddenly others began responding to me, sharing the symbol and their stories of other relatives they knew who had died or disappeared under strange circumstances. The symbol seemed to bond us together. We talk now through a private chat room—so the Guild won't find out about our plans to help others like her. That's why we came to look for you."

"How did you know we were here?"

"This is a small community. It is very easy to spot someone who doesn't belong here. Men from the Guild began patrolling this area ever since Ghazal died. They claimed to be police officers, but I grew up here. I know every police officer from this community. When the UWO convoy arrived in Kabul, the Guild's men questioned them. One of the UWO officers mentioned that two passengers were dropped off outside of Kabul. Your friend, Jalo, refused to tell them anything. They almost beat him to death, but another police officer, one who believes as I do, saved him.

"We hadn't seen the creatures in this area since Ghazal died, but suddenly they were back. We knew they must be looking for someone very special…a Seer like Ghazal. Like you…"

"We came here looking for her. Hoping she was alive. My sister is very sick. We were hoping that if she was alive, we could find a way to save her."

"I'm sorry, Liam, but I don't believe she is. People began reporting that they'd seen her, but that's not what I meant to happen. I meant she lives in those of us who know the truth and will stand with you. Her legacy saved lives. Even now, she is the reason we are here—to save your life so that you can save others. You can free others. Our sister will live my friend. No matter what happens, she will live on in each of us."

Alessandra had been awake for some time now, listening to the conversation between Fardeen and Liam. She knew Fardeen's words were true, but she also knew that Liam was not ready to accept them. When Liam did not respond, she spoke up.

"How many others like you are there?" She asked. Fardeen smiled down at her.

"In the chat room, we have over 200 members from France, Nigeria, the US...all over. I don't know how many others wear the mark as I do, but we all use it."

"Why?"

"So that you can identify us and know that you are safe."

●●∙∙●●

They had been moving across the Pass for two and a half days, only taking small breaks to eat, hide, and rest when absolutely necessary.

But despite every effort Liam and Fardeen had made, Alessandra still seemed to be growing weaker by the day. In the last twelve hours they had stopped four times to give Alessandra a chance to "catch her breath," which might have made sense if they weren't carrying her. When she wasn't catching her breath, she slept almost constantly.

Normally, Liam noted with increasing worry, she would have been able to heal herself, but for some reason he couldn't fathom, she wasn't able or willing to do that now. The only thing Liam had seen her eat or drink was water and a few bites of bread.

Whenever he would ask her what was wrong, she told him, "Nothing. I just need to reserve my energy," before drifting off to sleep. He checked her forehead for fever whenever she wouldn't swat his hand away.

"I'm fine," she'd mumbled to him just an hour ago. "I won't let anything happen. Please, Liam, you have to trust me."

Then why can't you heal yourself! He wanted to shout, but knew better.

Liam was beside himself with worry and the effort it took not to show it.

Over the last two weeks, they'd eaten the exact same things, he reasoned. There was no reason for whatever was ailing her to have escaped him, too.

To distract himself from madness, Liam walked over to Fardeen, who was peeling an orange at the other end of their camp. Fardeen offered him half as he sat down beside him.

"How long 'til we reach the bridge to Pakistan," Liam asked as he nodded his thanks and took a bite, letting the sweetness of the juice distract him from his thoughts.

"Another 12 hours, maybe a little more," Fardeen replied while purposefully keeping his eyes from where Alessandra sat, looking pale and sickly.

"The police officer I told you about, the one who saved your friend, his name is Anil. He has arranged for a colleague of his to meet us at the bridge. He will escort you into Pakistan, but we must leave soon. We must arrive before daylight."

"How much resistance do you think we'll encounter?" Liam asked.

"It's hard to say. If Anil's friend comes through, then hopefully very little, but nothing is certain."

"We don't have many weapons with us," Liam said aloud as he watched Alessandra try to stand, only to sit down again immediately. "She was so strong in the caves, but now…"

"A woman will do anything to protect her child," Fardeen said absently as he finished his orange.

Even the mention of it made it slightly hard for him to breath.

"No, we can't-" he started hoarsely. "The drugs they gave her…she doesn't-"

"I'm sorry," Fardeen said quietly, wishing he had kept his promise not to say anything about his suspicions. A few minutes passed before he thought of a way to bring their conversation back to safe territory.

Leaning his head in Alessandra's direction, Fardeen lowered his voice and asked, "Does she say anything about what will happen tomorrow?"

"No," Liam answered, shaking his head. "She just keeps saying that she needs to reserve her energy."

"Perhaps that's all we need to know. I think we should do the same."

By the time they were close enough to see the bridge, it was clear that Anil's friend had not been able to make a way for them. A barricade was erected 100 feet from the paved road that led to their side of the bridge. Liam counted at least 15 guards. Worse, search lights circled the perimeter, suggesting that somehow they knew Liam and Alessandra were coming.

"I'm sorry—we have to turn back," Fardeen whispered loud enough for the seven of them to hear. They lay flat on their bellies against the rocky hillside.

"No. We can make it."

All eyes turned to Alessandra who had been silent up until that moment.

"We can make it across, but we will have to move quickly. They are close by. Fardeen, you and your men will have to come with us. Join the rest of your family in Pakistan. It will not be safe to return here for several months. They know you've helped us."

Fardeen knew exactly what that meant.

"Anil?"

"I'm sorry," she said softly, allowing him only a moment of silence before she continued. "Help is coming for us, but first they need to know we're here. When I give the signal, I need you to throw one of your grenades into the barricade, then stay close behind us. Liam and I will lead you through, but first he needs one of your guns."

Fardeen motioned for one of the men to his right to pass Liam a rifle.

"What's the plan?" Liam asked, relieved to hear the strength in her voice. Looking at her face, she was the woman he saw in the cave again—fierce, determined, deadly.

"Do what you always do," she said with a slight smile. "Protect us."

Liam returned her smile as he checked his clip and got into firing position.

Upon her signal, Fardeen hurled the grenade into the barricade then fell back to the ground. The minute it exploded, Liam and Alessandra were on their feet. Liam returned fire as Alessandra extended her arms out to peel back the burning metal just before they ran through.

Once inside, Liam focused his assault on the Guard Tower behind them, while Alessandra cleared the path in front with pulses of energy that sent half a dozen guards flying over the bridge and down into the rocks below. The second wave of soldiers that came suffered the same fate, while Liam and Fardeen's men stopped the group that tried to close in on them from behind.

At both sides of the bridge, the last remaining soldiers prepared to focus their rocket launchers at the small group of them who were now trapped in the middle of the bridge.

"Alessandra, we can't stay here! They're going to blow the bridge," Liam yelled, looking back towards the path where they came. "Maybe we should…"

Before he could finish, he heard a helicopter approaching from behind, just before it began firing on the bridge. Alessandra's shield was up in an instant, surrounding them in a dome of blue liquid light. From inside its safety, Liam could barely believe what he was seeing. Instead of firing at them, the helicopter turned its guns on both guard towers and destroyed them before landing on the bridge. Ten men jumped out of the aircraft, running towards them quickly as a truck barreled through the gate at the opposite side of the bridge.

The men worked around them wearily, gathering dead bodies from the bridge. But Alessandra refused to lower her shield until Maura told her it was safe. As she did so, a woman in a pale grey stepped from the helicopter and walked with determined steps toward them.

"I prayed that somehow you would see me coming," she said in her thick Irish brogue. "But I didn't want to risk the operation, so I asked my Quorum to focus on blocking your sight until I could get to you."

"I knew help was coming, but I didn't know it was you," Alessandra responded.

"Deidra Pile?" Liam said in confusion.

"Yes," she said, accepting his skepticism while holding his gaze. "I meant what I said in Geneva. We will not survive this without your help. I've risked my life and the lives of many who are loyal to me to come here and prove it to you.

"But we don't have much time. I've suppressed the report that alerted this post to your arrival, but I don't know yet if it managed to get through to any other channels. The creatures found you once and they are always close, always searching for you. We need to leave now. My guards will stay and clean up the evidence of what happened here, but if the demons find us, I can't protect you. We need to go."

"Protect us! You sent those things to find us. You're the reason they knew we were here in the first place!" Liam said with contempt.

"No, I swear I didn't, but I know who did. My colleague, Andreas Menten has made some kind of alliance with them, and I need your help to stop him."

CHAPTER 16: THE QUIET

Liam sat quietly beside Alessandra in the helicopter, observing the dynamic between her and Deidra carefully. Alessandra seemed comfortable, but Liam still wasn't sure what to make of her, though he was grateful that she'd just saved their lives.

"I know you have no reason to trust me, so I appreciate your willingness to at least hear me out," Deidra began as she shifted her gaze between Alessandra and Liam.

"Your sister saved my life. I saw that thing pass over Andreas and come straight for me. That's when I knew that we had been betrayed from the inside. But it was only after I watched Andreas convince the remaining members of the Guild to turn the world against you as a means of appeasing these creatures that I knew what I had to do.

"I've been looking for you ever since. Each of you are top priorities on our watch list. We monitor every outlet—even internal reports when a Seer is gathered, looking for your whereabouts."

When Alessandra narrowed her eyes at her choice of words, Deidra quickly continued.

"Given what your sister went through to save me, and that she is the only other person besides Ghazal that we know of who has ever killed one of these things, I figured you would be very interested in the reports that Ghazal was still alive. We've been monitoring the area for several weeks now with no success of finding her.

"When I heard there was another attack by demons in this area, after weeks of no activity, I figured one of you must have been involved. At first, I thought you were dead, until the border patrol was contacted by a local police officer in Kabul about transporting an unidentified group of people from Afghanistan into Pakistan via the Khyber Pass. He thought he was talking to a friend in confidence, but we're always listening. He was tortured and killed by the time I got to him, but at least I was able to intercept the report before anyone else could find out where you were."

"So now what? You want our forgiveness for all the wrong you've done?" Liam sneered.

"Of course not," Deidra snapped. "Your forgiveness means as little to me as my regret does to you, young man. It won't save either of us. I came here to help. Tell me what you need to fight these things—to save us—and I'll get it for you."

Alessandra was silent as she let the Collective hear everything Deidra said through her own thoughts. When she returned her focus to the woman in front of her, she knew exactly what they needed from Deidra.

"We need every Seer you have within the Guild," Alessandra answered.

To her credit, Liam noted, Deidra didn't hesitate.

"How?"

"When you return home, there will be a package waiting for you. It contains a serum. All you'll need to do is get it into the Luridium supply that you distribute to the Seers The serum will help them access their full power."

"You mean all of them, not just the ones in Quorum?"

"Yes, it must be given to every Seer you have. Every single one of them."

Deidra's mind was already working out the logistical nightmare of making Alessandra's request feasible without getting caught immediately.

"Okay," Deidra answered pensively. But how will you get to them? I can't just give them the serum and release them."

"You won't need to, and the rest is not your problem to solve. If you want to help us, this is what you need to do."

Despite her doubts, Deidra knew there was only one way forward, and no turning back.

"I'll do whatever you need."

Deidra dropped Fardeen and his men off in Pakistan where his family had fled after Ghazal's death. Next, she left Liam and Alessandra at the border between India and Nepal. From there, they made their way to the monastery where Tenzen had grown up as a boy until he received the vision from Joel that compelled him to leave his home and travel to Iowa. By the time they reached the monastery, Alessandra had fallen ill again. The monks received them happily, as Tenzen had told them they would, and agreed with Liam that they should not leave until Alessandra was fully healed before they headed off to wherever they were needed next.

The healers that attended to Alessandra were helpful and kind, assuring him that all she needed was time. Liam gave her all the time he could that first night to bathe and rest as he wandered the ancient building alone, before finally entering their room to get some answers with the first morning light.

He carried their breakfast tray in quietly across the room to where her body was turned away from him on their bed—two single pallets pulled together under fresh sheets. There was a small table at the head of the bed with a glass of water and a few wooden sticks on a plate. Rather than disturb the arrangement, he put their tray at the foot of the bed and sat down on the floor.

She hadn't stirred and he didn't want to wake her, so he resolved to wait, feeling suddenly more nervous than desperate about the conversation they would have.

What he didn't know was that Alessandra was wide awake and waiting for him. Though the room was not big, the light from their large window made it feel a part of the great outdoors. While the sun had not yet risen, it was bright enough to see all the worry on Liam's face when she turned to him.

Alessandra put down the licorice root that had finally managed to settle her stomach and reached out her hand to him. Rather than rise to sit down beside her, he held her hand tighter as he rolled onto his knees, so that his face was only inches from hers.

"What's going on? I know you know. Please tell me."

"I will, Liam. I promise you, I'm fine. I just want to talk with you first about Lilli and what's happening to her. I want to know how you feel about that."

Immediately, Liam wanted to look away, but he couldn't. Her eyes held him, clear as if every light in the room was on. It was time they talked about it—past time if he was honest.

"I don't know. For most of the time we've been out here, I've been fighting it. Forcing myself to accept it one minute, then refusing to believe it the next. It feels like all my life has been about protecting her—keeping her alive—and now she's going to die and there's nothing I can do about it."

Alessandra watched him silently, unsure of what to say. Everything he said, she already knew, but she needed to hear his thoughts as much as he needed to admit them out loud.

"It was the last thing my mom ever told me," he continued. "The last thing she asked me to do. 'Go now. Protect Her.' That's all she said…"

"And you did that, Liam. You've done that."

"I know. I know that I've done everything I could do for her. I know that she's her own person now. She has to make her own choices. I can't do that for her anymore."

Liam looked down at Alessandra's fingers intertwined with his.

Wait for him, Alessandra told herself. *Wait.*

He traced the ridges in the palm of her hand for a long time before he spoke again.

"But, you know, what I said about my Mom. It's not true. That's not all she said to me. She told me about you, before I even met you. She told me she wanted me to have a family, to have a life of my own.

"I've been thinking about what Fardeen said about Ghazal, how he never got to say goodbye. How he never understood who Ghazal was until it was too late."

"Yes," Alessandra said drawing closer. "Go on."

"But that's not me. I know my sister. I know who she is and what she is. I've known it from since she was a kid—even when I didn't have a name for it, I knew. I've gotten to see the woman that she's become. I *helped* her become that person. I will get to say goodbye, but more than that, I get to be a part of her life now while she's still here.

As Liam paused, a small smile spread across her face as she watched him. She looked tired, he thought, tired but happy somehow. She nodded for him to continue.

"I was thinking of something else, too, while you were sleeping last night. I think I'm not just scared of losing her. We've been on the run so long; I've never had a plan. The chance to build my own life, I think the hope of that scares me sometimes—to see that far ahead. But Lilli's made her choice, and if we live through the end of this, *if* there is an end, I need to make mine."

"What do you want, Liam? What do you see?"

"I want to live," he said without hesitation. "I want to live with you and build some kind of life. I want to stop running and hiding and have a place, one place, that has all our stuff, like a closet and chairs and junk. I want us to live in a place long enough to have junk. I want to find a place or make a place that is safe enough to have kids."

When he saw the first of Alessandra's tears fall, he continued quickly.

"I know. I know, but we can adopt. We can just start picking up stray kids on the side of the road. It doesn't matter to me. I just want us to have a family—to be a family."

Alessandra smiled right through her tears as she took his face in her hands. She had wanted to tell him so many times in the past three weeks. Ever since she first realized what was happening to her, but there was too much chaos around them all to process the miracle of what she was about to tell him until he was ready—until right now.

"Do you want that, Alessandra? After everything that has happened, do you want that with me?"

"Yes, I want that, Liam. I love you."

"So tell me what's wrong? Tell me why you can't heal yourself the way you normally do. It's never taken this long before."

"I told you," she said, pulling him closer. "Nothing is wrong with me. It just might take a few months for me to feel better, but it's normal, what I feel. It's normal because we're going to have a baby."

Liam's mouth hung open so long, she could almost believe he didn't hear her, and when he finally did speak, she had to laugh.

"What!" He managed to say with the same stunned expression on his face. "I thought…"

"I don't know how. It's a miracle. You're going to be a father, Liam," she said as she placed their hands over her belly. "Our future is already here, Liam, and she's strong, so strong. She'll be stronger than all of us."

CHAPTER 17: BEFORE

Her smile was infectious.

"I'm going to be an aunt!" Lilli whispered into Joel's face as she drew him close.

"I know," he answered, pulling her even closer.

The metal floor beneath them clanked and clattered with every pebble and bump on the road. Two layers of blankets beneath them didn't make a bit of difference, but after three days, they were used to it.

"How do *you* know?" She teased, laughing into his neck as he kissed her.

"I know because *you* know." The notion made them both chuckle.

She traced the outline of his cheekbones as their laughter died down.

"Liam's going to be a great father," she said after a while.

"Yes, he is. A bit overprotective, but he can't help himself, can he?"

She drew closer still until their lips touched.

Though it had been a perilous journey, everything that had happened was going according to plan, exactly how they had seen it, despite the interference the demons caused in their visions.

In Geneva, the meeting goal had been to claim the one person who could give them access to every Seer in the Guild. While it took more time than they had anticipated for her to become truly proactive, Deidra was now in place, carrying out a part of the plan. Eli's findings had also been critical. Once they analyzed the sites where the demons attacked most frequently, they found that they corresponded almost exactly with every Seer who was scheduled to be gathered by the Guild, and therefore rescued by the Lost Seers.

Neva's theory on this correlation was that the demons were in essence carrying out an insurance policy to strike at their ability to recruit any more Seers who would develop the power to kill them. Neva concluded that the secondary consequence of inadvertently reducing the Guild's access to Seers did not seem to be something they were concerned about given the greater threat more powerful Seers presented to their survival. As a result, the Seers were able to focus their efforts and save more Seers from falling into the Guild's hands.

Hasaam and Ngozi's DNA analysis also helped them understand exactly what the Seers were up against every time they confronted one of the demons. On a molecular level, the demons' blood and flesh samples revealed that their entire bodies seemed to be made up of a hybrid stem cell with an indestructible mitochondria that allowed their cells to be in a permanent state of regeneration and mutation. Ngozi concluded that the cell mutation process might explain how they were able to disguise themselves in human form. It also suggested that this function might also give them the ability to mimic other human forms, appearing as anyone if need be. The knowledge helped them to use Maura and Lilli's abilities more effectively in every fight in which the Collective engaged.

Even the initiation of Lilli's transcendence brought about a breakthrough that would not have been possible otherwise, providing the missing link that would unite all the Seers together when the time came.

It gave them comfort when they thought about all the people who had suffered and all the Seers who would die to know that every sacrifice was for a purpose, a reason that was greater than everything that would be lost.

It made them grab on to every piece of joy they could.

"Can you see her?" Lilli asked shyly. She had tried many times, but her excitement precluded any hope of objectivity.

"Yeah," he said smiling higher. "She's beautiful."

"What does she look like?" She asked, tickling his ribs with her fingers. "Tell me!"

Instead of answering, he closed his eyes, letting the images fill his thoughts. Lilli soaked them up greedily until she came to several images of her niece as an adult.

"She looks like all of us?" Lilli said with a gasp. "How is that possible?"

"I have no idea," Joel whispered. His voice shared her awe, her joy, as he said again, "I have no idea."

They reveled happily in Joel's memory of the future until they felt the truck they had stowed away in slow down.

They were close. The irony of where they were headed did not escape them. To be back in Chicago again—the place where they first met—was, in a way, fitting.

The city that had once been a beacon of beauty was in ruins, abandoned and evacuated by all who were able to leave. The stakes were high then and even higher now. Millennium Park had been turned into a refugee camp of sorts, a way station for Seers and sympathizers to be gathered and sorted on their way to a Purification Center, death, or both. The Guild called them Quarantine Stations, and the one in Chicago was the largest of its kind in the Northern Hemisphere—a place you only came if you were dragged there. Unlike most of the other stations, this one was guarded by both men and demons, though the Guild claimed they were random attacks whenever a demon managed to kill a prisoner. The demons took pleasure in making examples out of those who had the audacity to resist when they were captured—or so the rumors told. It would not be long before Joel and Lilli, along with the rest of the Seers, found out for themselves.

The truck slowed to a stop as the driver pulled over on the side of the only highway still open to the city.

They got to their feet quickly. Joel used the narrow light peeking through the steel doors to unlock the motorcycle that they carried with them, while Lilli stretched her limbs, assessing her strengths and weaknesses. She was stronger than she had been a couple weeks ago, as strong now as she would ever be in the in-between place where she existed. Besides the backpack that Lilli was fastening securely to her shoulders, they carried nothing else with them.

The door swung open to reveal the same spectacled man Lilli had first met at Heathrow Airport in London. Above the rims of his fine wire glasses, his brow was heavy with concern as he lowered the ramp that Joel would use to roll their bike to the ground.

"I wish I could convince ya to turn around," the escort said. "There's nothing but death inside there, especially for you. Don't need to see the future to know that."

Joel smiled and drew him into a wordless hug. Lilli watched in silence as their embrace lingered.

"Thanks for everything," Joel said as he pulled away and got on his bike with Lilli.

"The name is Horace," he replied. "Horace Sands, and it's been an honor. When you call me again, you can call me by my name, ya hear?"

"I always do, Horace," Joel grinned as the bike beneath them roared to life. "I always do."

They gave Horace one final wave before turning their sights to the road ahead. When the city was alive, the drive from the Chicago suburbs where Horace had left them to downtown Chicago would have taken an hour, but now, with no one around for miles, it would take them less than 30 minutes. The cameras that would have tracked their every move were blinded as Lilli bent the light around them to make their approach invisible.

As her mind raced forward to get a clearer sense of what was coming, she couldn't escape the horror of what her visions showed her. She was glad that Joel couldn't see it through her mind, though she was sure he felt the dread in her heart as he pushed down on the accelerator.

"Are you afraid?" She asked, holding him tighter as if to shield him from what was about to happen to them and all the other Seers in position at other Quarantine Centers around the world who were ready to do exactly what they were about to.

"No." His voice held so much conviction that she could feel the words vibrate through his chest as he spoke. Joel took one hand from the motorcycle bar and intertwined it with hers.

"The only thing that I'm afraid of is losing you."

CHAPTER 18: THE STORM

They had never tried anything like it before—an all-out global assault on every Quarantine Station the Guild had with every Seer who was old enough to fight. The entire plan took less than 24 hours to execute, but for each of the Seers who survived, it felt like a large fraction of eternity.

For weeks, they had tried to fight with caution, fending off individual attacks and rescuing as many people as they could from the Quarantine Stations, but the death toll had become too high. For every group they saved, the demons, working with Andreas and the Guild, killed dozens, sometimes hundreds more in retaliation, trying to snuff out cries of resistance from a population that was beginning to question their motives. In the media, the Guild always washed their hands of blame, claiming it was the refusal of the Seers to surrender that caused the unnecessary bloodshed.

But while the Guild continued to distort reality in the press, a different story was slowly taking shape on the ground as more and more people saw the Seers risk their lives to save others. Slowly, a pattern of stories began to emerge of communities coming under attack only to have their cries for help ignored by local authorities until a group of people they did not know came to fight on their behalf. In each case, the Seers were the ones who came offering food, supplies, and other assistance while the authorities blamed the community for bringing the attacks upon themselves by harboring Seers in the first place.

As the stories spread, communities began to recognize the Seers as the only solution to defeating the demons that terrorized them. Slowly, people began seeking out ways to help the Seers in any way they could, identifying themselves by the same symbol Ghazal had given Fardeen before she died.

For the Seers, the shift was profound, bringing new life to their efforts. They could finally stop defending themselves from the very people they were trying to save. But the change was not enough to turn the tide.

Their inability to predict the exact location or outcome of an attack, combined with the simple fact that they were outnumbered on every front, with too many people to save on one side and too many forces against them on the other, made fighting, winning, or even staying alive nearly impossible on any given day.

So they decided to do the only thing they could: confront the threat were they knew it would be most heavily concentrated.

If there was ever a chance of changing their fate, this was it.

● ○ · · ○ ●

It began in Chicago, where the Quarantine Station looked more like a prison than the elegant outdoor park it had once been. Plastic tents, latrines and cots were scattered like litter across the dimly lit space. Water and food were so scarce that people were forced to fish, bathe, and drink from the unfiltered waters of Lake Michigan to survive. There were well over a thousand people in this makeshift facility alone, most of whom the Guild knew couldn't be Seers. There just weren't enough Seers in the general population to have amassed such a large number so quickly. But the image of them all together served to amplify the idea that the problem of the Seers was everywhere and that the consequences of harboring one of them were severe.

Lilli and Joel slipped past the main checkpoint unseen, within the cloak of light that Lilli provided. Once inside the perimeter, Lilli disarmed the security alarm and had the gate of the Quarantine Station open before anyone knew they were there. Her main job was to lead those inside to the subway station and barricade them inside, while Joel held off the soldiers until she returned. By then, the demons would have gathered and they could take them on together.

Once the gate was open, Lilli unfolded the light around her and appeared before the crowd. Every conversation around her seemed to stop at once as the crowds' attention was drawn first by the mysterious opening of the gate and next by a girl appearing out of nowhere.

"Please, don't move. My name is Lilith Knight and I am here to help you." Lilli could already see one man about to make a run for the gate. She tried again.

"Please, listen to me! All of you. Do not make any sudden movements. Even though you can't see them, they are very close and we don't want to draw their attention. We don't have much time before the creatures discover that Joel and I are here. We can get you out safely, but you have to trust me."

Everyone knew who she was. They had seen her likeness on the news more times than they cared to remember. They just weren't sure if they were ready to disbelieve everything they had heard.

"Where will you take us? There's no place we can hide." A woman asked from across the field. Though she stood as still as her shaking body would allow, her voice carried clear and strong.

"You're going to run to the subway station just two blocks away from here. Once we're there. I will barricade you in. The trains aren't running in the city anymore, so you can travel underground. Take the tunnels. Split up in two groups, one toward Richton Park, the other towards Aurora. At the end of each line, someone will be waiting to help you with the things you need."

"Two blocks!" A man blurted out from the crowd. "Did you miss all the bodies they left to rot on the way in here? They thought they could make it, too." The man started to move towards her before another man caught his arm and stilled him.

"You will make it," Lilli said calmly.

"How do you know?" The man standing closest to her asked.

"Because I've seen it."

"Well if you've seen all this, how come you weren't smart enough to escape? How come you ended up here with us?" The first man spat bitterly. Lilli stared at him for a moment before smiling sadly.

"I didn't come here to escape. I came here for you."

Her answer seemed to be the one he needed to hear because as soon as she moved back towards the gate, everyone moved with her.

But he was right about one thing. They didn't make it two feet out of the gate before the tower guard noticed the activity behind him and moved to sound the alarm. But Joel was already on him before his hand could reach the red button, rendering him unconscious with a blow to the head.

They made it another 150 feet before they heard the sound that every heart dreaded: A distant screeching that seemed to swallow up the last bit of light in the sky.

"Move! Move!" Lilli yelled as she pushed the concrete barriers out of their way with a wave of her hand. Stepping to the side, she urged them on as they rushed past.

"Straight ahead. You can make it! Run!"

They were well out of the compound before Lilli heard Joel blow up the first of the tanks that had rolled in to follow them. She looked back to find his shield projected out behind the crowd she was now leading, protecting a mother and her two children from the shrapnel that was about to descend. Lilli picked up the bigger of the two children, the one who reminded her most of Joel when he was a boy, hugged him tightly, and ran.

●　●　·　·　●　●

No one was left to face him except the ones for whom he was waiting. The guards who were still alive had all ran off after realizing that they didn't have the firepower to stop him if he chose to turn his will on them. Those who refused to accept that fact were dead.

The screeching of their approach surrounded him and for a second, he was glad that Lilli wasn't with him yet. For a moment, he could pretend she was underground where it was safe—even if he knew it wasn't true.

He could feel her breathing fast, like a murmur in his own lungs as she came closer. Since her recovery, she had learned to measure the pace of her thoughts to his as a means of keeping her grounded to this side of life. He could hear her clearly now as she ran the last block back to him.

They're close, hiding. I can feel them around us. There are more of them, more than I thought.

He turned his body fully to where he could just make out the faint image of her coming closer. Behind her loomed a cluster of tall, desolate buildings. The windows of hotels and offices that had once been lit from inside now stood like corpses who had permanently shut their eyes to the evil they could no longer bear to witness. The clouds above her bellowed like smoke rising off the fading sun.

As if the world is on fire, he thought and he could feel it too—the battle that had already begun for others in the Collective. He prayed that they would all survive even though he knew they wouldn't.

Joel heard the glass breaking before he saw it, like slivers of ash falling down as they caught the last light of day. But the sound of wings extending out was familiar to him. He'd been listening for it since they'd arrived.

By the time Lilli turned around to see three of the demons overhead, Joel had already decided what to do. The chain link fence behind him groaned and snapped as it ripped from the ground. He sent it flying into the air, wrapping it around the three demons above her before they could escape. With each turn of the fence length around them, he cinched it tighter until they were clawing each other for air. Before they hit the ground, Joel hurled them into the river.

When Lilli finally got to him, there were four more approaching from the left and another two from behind. In a matter of seconds, they would be surrounded.

The fight lasted longer than either of them would have believed they were physically capable of sustaining. Since their last fight with the demons, Joel and Lilli had learned how essential it was to stay physically connected in order to combine and share their abilities as efficiently as possible. But after the first hour of fighting, the demons understood this as well and tried to drive them apart as often as they could.

They also learned that eliminating the demons' wings helped to level the playing field for a little while, but ultimately there was no maneuvering that could outweigh the fact that the demons were stronger, faster, and seemingly incapable of being mortally wounded. In the hours before dusk arrived, both Joel and Lilli had reached the limits of their bodies' ability to recover from injury.

As exhausted and battered as they were, they refused to draw any energy from within the Collective, where Seers were fighting and dying with a frequency they were too heartbroken to calculate. While there were at least twice as many Seers at any other Quarantine location where the Seers fought, Joel and Lilli had wanted it that way. Among every Seer within the Collective, it was understood that no one could do what Joel and Lilli could do on their own, and that others needed the numerical advantage more than they did.

But even they could not hold out forever, and after hours of exhaustion, the demons finally succeeded in separating them with a blow to the chest that sent Joel flying into the air. If Lilli had not caught him, he would have died the instant he hit the ground, but the distraction cost her dearly as another demon crashed into her, leaving her disoriented for only a moment. But it was enough to have two demons poised and ready to rip her apart before she heard a voice pierce the air.

"Stop!"

She knew immediately from the timbre and echo in his voice what he had done. All voices within the Collective went silent as they felt Joel move past their consciousness.

The demons dropped their claws from her immediately—hissing and snapping at their inability to control their actions. Talons gouged the concrete beneath their feet as they turned to Joel unwillingly.

"Die," he said simply, but his voice reverberated through the open space as if amplified.

To Lilli it seemed that the entire field filled with screams as the two demons in front of them burst into flames, their flesh slowly melting away to revel the charred bodies of a man and a woman who stood for a moment, frozen in death, before collapsing to the ground in a pile of ash. Between them stood Joel glowing and vibrant like a god, with the light of the sun behind him.

He turned to feel the other demons around him and seek them out, but his search was met with silence. All around were the charred remains of those they had managed to capture and restrain as well as others they had just been fighting moments ago. In the sky, he could just make out two that had managed to escape, two out of the 18 they had been fighting all night. With a calmness and certainty he had never felt before, he turned back to Lilli and reached out for her hand.

"Are you all right?" He asked tenderly, but his voice still shook the air.

"Yes," she said in awe of how magnificent it was to witness his transcendence.

"How did you…?" She began before she simply set her mind free to match his.

We have to gather them. Bring them to us, then say the words, they thought in unison.

How long do we have? He asked, wondering already how much he should resist the compulsion to release all the energy he felt bursting open from inside.

You need to resist it, but I don't think we have long. We know what we have to do now. We don't have a choice.

Yes, he agreed as they made their way back to the bike that had gotten them there. *There's only one thing left to do.*

CHAPTER 19: A REASONABLE MAN

The news report began with a video of Joel standing in front of the camera, reading a prepared speech.

"To avoid the devastation and bloodshed that we now see we are powerless to stop, myself and every member of our Collective are prepared to surrender to the Guild in exchange for the immediate closure of every Quarantine Station and the release of every person who is not a Seer within these facilities.

"We will take the next 48 hours to say goodbye to our loved ones and come to terms with the uncertainty ahead. Until our surrender, we urge everyone to stay indoors to remain as safe as possible before our surrender. In two days' time, each of us will make ourselves known in whatever location we choose. You will be free at that time to do with us what you will. We place our faith in your word and hope that our surrender will finally put an end to all the suffering these creatures have caused."

Deidra watched the video with the rest of the world, with no warning and no understanding of what it meant.

Her only clue was the delivery she received at her office this morning, a box with a syringe filled with fluid that looked like the serum that had been delivered to her door weeks ago and a note inside that read "For You." As far as Deidra was concerned, those were no clues at all.

She had done everything they had asked of her. Despite a worldwide distribution system that was obsessively guarded and monitored, she had managed to get the serum into each of the three Luridium production plants under the guise of an impromptu quality inspection. As the third highest officer in the Guild, it was not unheard of for someone of her rank to inspect the facilities personally, but it was rare for any official to arrive alone.

However, once she got inside, the process of contaminating the Luridium supply was shockingly simple. All she had to do was inject one of the three vials into the production chamber within each facility. While the radioactive components of the drug necessitated weekly production due to the unstable nature of the compound, the psychotropic components of Luridium were much more stable, allowing them to be developed and stored ahead of the need to synthesize. The stable component was maintained in its liquid form and stored in vats. At each facility, Deidra found a moment to slip away or come back late at night in one case. Each Guild member had their own access code to the production facilities. As long as no one checked the access log, there wouldn't be anything to suspect.

I can't be blamed for vigilance, Deidra tried to convince herself as she boarded her private plane back to Geneva. Though Deidra had never been homesick in the thousands of times she'd travelled away from the Purification Center she ran in Glasgow or her hometown of Belfast, she found herself missing both of those places now that she knew what it meant to be utterly alone. Though she played the role to the height of her ability, she had ceased to be a member of the Guild the moment she saw Lilli save her life and kill that demon at the same time.

In her more than two decades with the Guild, she had always been convinced that she was on the right side of history. She had no illusions about what they did as an organization. She understood the Guild's operation for what it was, an atrocity. But sometimes, she reasoned atrocities were necessary. In Deidra's mind, most people were unwilling to make the hard choices, not out of confusion over which way to choose, but out of simple fear of judgment or blame, insecurities Deidra had always risen above.

At less than one percent of the world's population, their enslavement seemed to be a small price to pay for all the benefits their gift could provide around the world. She had easily accepted being the villain for what she believed was the greater good. But the demons changed all of that.

After the meeting in Geneva, it was clear to her that the greater good could only be served by those who could help them survive. If allegiances needed to be changed, then so be it. At heart, Deidra had always been a pragmatist. But the change in perspective didn't make her one of the Seer sympathizers either, who she considered to be idiots.

How do you expect to help anyone when you throw up your symbols like bloody targets on your forehead, she'd thought to herself more than once in disgust.

To Deidra, the most powerful allies were always hidden, and that's what she'd tried to be ever since she received Alessandra's package three weeks ago. And that made her outside of everything for the first time in her life.

So Joel's newest video announcing their surrender left her baffled and slightly afraid. If they failed, there was no alternative, no escape.

"How could they give up?" She muttered to herself as she paced. She knew the fighting at the Quarantine Stations had been bloody, but blood was to be expected. Death was to be expected. "If they can't defeat them, then…"

"I see you've heard the good news," Andreas said slyly as he stood in the doorway to her office.

How long has he been standing there? Deidra wondered as she tried not to let her surprise show.

Deidra stopped pacing immediately and perched herself on the corner of her desk.

"Yes, I heard, though I don't know if I'd call it good news."

"Why on Earth not?" Andreas replied smugly. "We have what we've always wanted: the Lost Seers back under our grasp and peace at last in the world. You should be pleased."

"Yes, I would be if it were all those things, Andreas, but I've yet to see a representative come forth from one of these creatures to offer any of the assurances you presume. I have yet to see how giving them what they want ensures we get to survive."

Deidra appraised him carefully as she considered her next words. She and Andreas had not been friends or seen eye-to-eye on anything in years. This was not a social call.

If he needed something from me, he would have asked for it already, she reasoned.

The nonchalance with which he strolled around her office gave it away. Deidra could tell he knew something. The only reason he was in her office was either to gloat or to interrogate. If it was the latter, it meant that he thought he knew something about her.

The only way I'll know for sure is to find out, she thought before clearing her throat.

"But then again, perhaps you have the inside track on things. Maybe you've come to share?" She asked.

Andreas had circled his way back to her front door and closed it. Deidra swallowed hard.

"Perhaps," Andreas answered as she heard him turn the lock.

He just admitted it! She could feel her body run cold with fear, but she forced herself to speak.

"Is there something you're going to tell me that can only be said behind lock and key?"

"Oh, yes," he said, turning back to her with a smile, "But first, you're going to tell me something."

Deidra could feel the strength of her entire body dissolve.

He knows, she thought in desperation. *He knows.* Then she caught herself.

If he was certain, I'd be dead already. He's just trying to intimidate me into giving myself away, she reasoned.

Deidra forced herself up by her arms and made her way casually to the bar.

"Oh, I've been trying to tell you things for years now, Andreas. I'd all but given up on your education. This could take a while. Do you want a drink?" Andreas nodded cautiously. Deidra could feel his eyes on her, tracking her every move.

She poured the scotch into two glasses with an even hand and passed it to him with a smile. They drank in silence, watching each other over the rims of their tumblers before continuing.

Andreas reached down into his jacket pocket, pulled out a small syringe and held it up between them.

"Do you know what this is?" He asked. His tone was calm, but his smile was gone.

Deidra looked at it closely with feigned interest before staring back at him in amusement.

"The source of all your delusions," she said, before finishing the scotch in her hand.

"No, Deidra. I wish it was, but it's not. It's Luridium, but not the one you tampered with; this is a new batch we administered to the Seers today. Whatever you had planned is over."

It took all of Deidra's courage to balk in his face.

"Oh dear, you are delusional! Why would I tamper with the Luridium supply?"

"I don't know. I was going through the activity logs of our Guild members..."

Deidra cocked her eyebrow in response, cutting him off momentarily.

"It's my job as the newly appointed Chairman of the Guild to monitor the whereabouts of each of our members. These are dangerous times, Deidra. I can't protect you if I don't know where you are."

"I wasn't aware I needed protection," Deidra answered doubtfully, but Andreas pressed on.

"I know you were there, Deidra, at each of our production facilities three weeks ago."

"Yes and what of it?" Her voice rose with indignation. "Doesn't the Chair of the Guild have anything better to do than monitor my every move?"

She used the moment to put some distance between them as she returned to the bar.

Ignoring her accusation, Andreas continued.

"I asked them to test a sample of the supply. At first they couldn't see any difference and then they did a routine ultraviolet scan and nothing showed up. The scanner couldn't identify a single chemical in it except for hemoglobin. There were traces of blood in the sample."

"Well it's not mine, I assure you!"

"They couldn't identify the blood type. They think it's mutated somehow. The samples before you arrived were fine."

"Mutated blood? I see. And where would I get ahold of that? Seems more likely that you need tech support." Seizing the flash of doubt in his eyes, Deidra went on.

"Look Andreas, I don't know what this is about. While you and the rest of your sycophants have been fretting over press coverage of a band of Seer sympathizers, someone had to look out for our vulnerabilities. I visited our production centers to make sure the base of our control was secure, something you might have thought to do when you were a reasonable man."

Something shifted then in Andreas' expression. She couldn't say what it was, but it frightened her.

"I don't need to be reasonable," Andreas said calmly. "Now, I have power."

Deidra made her way over to the opposite side of her desk, the farthest point from him that she could get to without backing herself into a corner.

"Power over what, a world that's falling apart?"

"Why didn't you tell us about the sighting in Afghanistan?"

That caught her off guard. She had been so careful, but apparently not careful enough.

"There was nothing there. I got the report en route to the Quarantine Station in Calcutta and changed course to investigate the report myself. When I got there, there was nothing. Nothing! In case you hadn't noticed, site reports from that part of the world aren't too reliable. They're still claiming that the Afghan girl is still alive, and that hasn't turned up any warm bodies, either."

For a second he looked as if he was considering her words. She'd kept her voice indignant, but not shrill, biting and sarcastic, but soundly logical. She was utterly herself. She couldn't do anything more to convince him.

But then his eyes shifted back to hers and she knew there was nothing of the reasonable man she once knew inside him.

"The thing is, I just can't trust you, Deidra. I just can't." He stepped towards her slowly with the syringe of Luridium rising in his hand.

"Stop, Andreas! You don't have to do this. You can trust me. We both serve The Guild." Deidra was rounding the desk as he cut off her path to the door.

"I'm just so close, so close to everything I've ever wanted, and you're just not on my side. You don't see."

Deidra almost felt sad for the man he used to be.

"You're going to die with the rest of us, Andreas. No matter what they promised you."

They paused then, staring at each other from opposite sides of the table.

"Maybe," he said, finally looking calm and rational once more. Deidra let out a shaky breath. "But you first."

Before she had a chance to react, he grabbed the sleeve of her suit jacket and pulled her towards him across the desk.

Her arms flailed wildly as she tried to catch hold of anything that could stop him or help her get away, but it was too late. Andreas jammed the syringe into the side of her neck with such force that her forehead split open on the marble surface of her desk.

It wasn't in her nature to scream. As the needle cut through the back of her throat like a knife, she tried to hold onto the edge of the desk, tried to bear it, tried to fight.

He left her there, holding onto the desk until her arms gave out. When she fell, she took half the contents on her desk with her. By the time she rolled on her stomach the nausea had already begun. Her skin felt like it was on fire.

"I can't give up," she rasped. "If I can get help..."

She meant to make it across the room, but couldn't manage more than a foot. In front of her, propped neatly open, was the strange box she received this morning. There was a note taped to the bottom that she could read perfectly from her vantage point on the ground.

"For you," it read. The syringe was just within reach.

CHAPTER 20: FROM PRAGUE TO PARIS

Alessandra didn't know if it was providence or mercy that made the gathering before her possible. Somehow the ones that mattered most to her had all survived the awful night that took so many from them—too many. She was just getting to know Mai and Ammon. Pytor, she thought, might have been a good friend in a place where there was time to make good friends. She would never get to say goodbye to Tess, Eric, Jared, or Emma. The heartbreak of losing them all in one night stole her breath away when she lingered on it.

But she didn't want to hold them at the forefront of her memory right now. She wanted to enjoy the moment for as long as she could, because in the morning they would head out to do the last thing any of them could do to finally stop the madness around them.

"More, please! Have more. There is plenty." Alessandra smiled as she watched Mrs. Patashka flutter around the room.

When they came back together to decide where to spend their final night together, the choice had been obvious. Mrs. Patashka welcomed them with tears and open arms just as Maura had said she would. They sat around the candle lit tables with the shades drawn tight. As with the last time, Joel assured them that they should be safe for the night, but as always, nothing was certain.

●●··●●

In a few hours they would ride from Prague to Paris. Most spent the previous day in personal pursuits, savoring the things they thought they would miss most. For Joel, that meant spending the day working with Alessandra, Ngozi, Hasaam, Neva, and Eli to ensure that everything was in place to continue the Restoration Project, while Liam and Lilli spent the afternoon together.

The first Restoration Project volunteers had finished their full cycle of treatment and had already begun experiencing glimpses of the future on their own. Some had even begun training to control their visions in Quorum. Alessandra would be responsible for continuing their training and leading the Restoration Project in Joel's absence. With all of them by her side, Alessandra finalized the legal document that gave her control over Renoit's estate and the Restoration Projects assets.

While Joel said his goodbyes to the team that had brought him so far, Liam and Lilli travelled to a small lake just outside the city where they could enjoy the quiet of the countryside. Sitting across from each other in their tiny boat, they were a long way from Hunt, Texas, but neither of them cared.

Looking at her, Liam had a hard time believing that this was one of the last times he would see Lilli. She looked absolutely radiant. Her skin seemed to be infused with light which made her hand in his look almost golden.

"So, are you going to name her after me?" Lilli giggled. Her fishing pole lay at the bottom of the boat, untouched.

Liam tried his best to return her laugh, but said nothing. It hurt him deeply to think of the fact that Lilli would never meet his daughter, never see her face.

"That's not true, you know," she said, picking up on his thoughts. "I already know what she's going to look like, and she has my ear," Lilli announced proudly.

"Your ear?" Liam repeated doubtfully.

"Yes, my left one. The good one."

"And the right?" He asked smiling despite himself.

"Oh, that's not my fault. I have no idea who she got that one from."

Liam laughed out loud, a rolling belly-filling laughter that no one but Lilli could bring out in him. When he finally caught his breath, he was still smiling.

"You're determined to get me in a good mood, aren't you?"

"It's my job to be silly. I'm your little sister," Lilli teased.

She was and she wasn't, he thought, but he didn't say it out loud.

"It's hard to believe sometimes."

Lilli studied him for a minute, then smiled.

"Do you remember what I told you when we returned from Chicago, the first time you met Joel?"

"You said we would never be apart, that the distance between us did not exist."

"That's still true. It will always be true. You won't be able to see me in the same way you do now, but I will always be here."

"But I won't be able to talk to you, to hear your voice, to know that you're okay." The tears came quickly though he tried to hold them back.

Lilli got up and hugged him tightly as he cried. She tried to make herself as solid as she could, as solid as he would remember.

"You will know that I'm okay, Liam. I promise. I promise."

"I'm proud of you, you know," she whispered then. "I'm proud of the choices you've made, of the life you're going to live."

"I'm proud of you, too. Of the woman you've become," Liam whispered back." Of all the sacrifices you've made to serve this world, to make it a better place. None of this would be possible without what you've done. I hope my daughter grows up to be a woman like you."

"Ohhhhh…" Lilli groaned as she felt her own tears begin to flow. "Stop it! Stop it! You're not supposed to make me cry, too."

"I'm your big brother. It's my job to make you cry," he said, tugging a lock of her hair playfully.

"I still hate that," she said as she pulled away half-laughing and half-crying at the memory of Liam sneaking up behind her as a child to pull her hair while she played with her favorite stuffed animals. Their mother would march him off to the corner every time, but Liam never cared. He'd just stick his tongue out at her while she pouted. They watched each other with sad-happy eyes. The sun was setting and it was time to head back.

"I love you," he said to her as the last tear fell from his eyes. "Nothing will ever change that."

"No, it won't," Lilli agreed while her tears still ran free.

They made their way back to the city just in time for a very special dinner in Prague.

Maura and Tenzen arrived late and stay pressed together at the very corner of their table. Looking at the tender way in which Tenzen kissed each of Maura's fingers as they wrapped around his gave everyone the grace not to ask what had taken them so long to get there.

Rachel and Marshall were there as well, though they would not make the trip afterwards. Rachel was finally ready to begin the restoration process with Vincent, and Joel had insisted that Marshall stay to play an important role in the rebuilding to come. To Alessandra, the room around her was full with laughter and tears and a dozen tiny, intimate conversations. Everything their life had been since Marcus first spoke to her in Crane's office a lifetime ago was there. Closing her eyes, she could almost imagine them at the commune during one of their social nights. Liam would be playing chess with Kaido, who was secretly pretending to be drunk so that he could let Liam win. Lucia would be whispering a dirty joke to Lilli who would turn red in the face by the ideas that sparked in her brain. Maura would be telling stories to the babies who refused to go to sleep while Katia let herself, for just a moment, pretend to be one of them. Kyle and Jared would be sitting close to them hoping as always to get noticed.

Hanna would be sampling Rachel's pastries and Jean's beignets. Rachel would be in deep conversation with Eli, Eric, and Tess, while Marshall stood by patiently waiting for the love that she would eventually give him. And Marcus would be sitting, listening intently while somehow still keeping watch over all of them to make sure they were safe.

Throughout the evening each of them had come up to Alessandra, laid their hands on her stomach, and given their daughter a blessing. Maura had given her discernment so that she would always know her friends from her enemies. Katia had blessed her with strength. Joel's gift was compassion for herself and her fellowmen. And when it came to Lilli's turn, she simply wished her love. Alessandra could feel the power of their words penetrate her skin and knew their gifts would be made real, that each of them would become a part of her child.

Closing her hands around her belly she promised herself that her daughter would know them all, the people who were here tonight and everyone who'd been taken from them too soon.

By the time she opened her eyes, Liam was beside her, back from hovering over Joel and his sister. He didn't know how to say goodbye, and it was too soon for him to realize that he didn't have to.

"What were you thinking?" He asked, brushing the side of her cheek before he sat down and stole a chunk of meat from the goulash on her half-eaten plate.

"How grateful I am for this moment and for what each of them has meant to my life. I will miss them so much."

"Me, too," Liam answered. "Me, too."

● ◦ ‧ ◦ ●

By the time they headed out, it was after midnight. Mrs. Patashka packed containers of her goulash for each of them, despite their insistence that it wasn't necessary. But they took them anyway because they knew she'd been cooking ever since she got Maura's call to make sure that, this time, she wouldn't run out of food.

On impulse, Mrs. Patashka had scrawled the Seer symbol onto her front door to show them in meaning what she could not say with words. But she never intended for it to have the effect that it did. As she slowly opened her front door, there were candles everywhere, on the steps to her restaurant and street curbs, leading out for as far as the eye could see. People lined the streets in silence. Some held candles in their hands while others displayed signs or tattoos. Everywhere she looked, there was the same symbol she had placed on her door. *These people have come,* she realized, *to thank them.* Looking back into the restaurant, she saw her guests observing the crowd outside with gratitude. One-by-one, they kissed her on the cheek and got into their vehicles. No one spoke a word. There was no need.

●•••●●

Joel led them out with Lilli on the fastest bike he could get his hands on. He kept it quiet on the way out of town, rolling at a steady pace. But once they hit the open road, he let it roar. The drive from Prague to Paris was supposed to take just over nine hours, but Joel had a much shorter trip in mind. He planned to beat the sun before its rays illuminated the first brick in the gloomy collection of broken buildings and dust that Paris had become. As one of the cities that had been completely demolished in the fight they had waged against the demons, it suited their purposes perfectly. They needed a place that was largely deserted for their plan to work.

The others rode behind him. Maura and Tenzen were to his right on a bike similar to his, with Liam and Alessandra to his left in a drop-top Jeep. Behind them Katia, Michael, and Nina each had motorcycles of their own.

The night was frigid but none of them felt it. Inside, they were on fire. The sky grew dense around them as the cities and towns they drove through fell away. With travel still severely restricted on most thoroughfares, they took over the road, spreading out and letting the darkness encase them as they let their fears, worries, and doubts fall away.

Alessandra started first, turning up the Jeep's sound system with Massive Attacks' "Unfinished Sympathy," a song she knew Liam loved—the only song that could possibly match their pace.

As soon as she heard the opening notes, Maura turned back to look at Alessandra with the most wicked smile she'd ever thought to see on such a sweet girl's face. In the next instant, Maura tore off her jacket, threw it up in the air, and lit it on fire. Her body began to glow. Nina was next, whooping and howling and dancing as she went. By the time Michael, Tenzen, and Katia joined in, hats, gloves, wool coats, and scarves had turned to nothing more than ribbons of light in the sky as their bodies swayed to the music, shimmering and glowing in the night that was now not nearly so dark.

Liam felt his own smile take over as he watched the girl beside him shake and groove to the music he knew she'd chosen just for him, the same girl who had once asked him shyly to teach her how to dance. Inside, he knew something precious was ending, but like the others, he was beginning to understand that something important, maybe even beautiful, was starting too, and that each of them had played a part in it. And though he couldn't fathom the next chapter of his life, he was suddenly sure of one thing; like the child growing in his wife's belly, it was worth living for.

Lilli was the last to remove the hoodie that covered her hair. Unzipping it, the material seemed to melt away from her skin in a mist of ashes and embers. She could feel the anticipation in the Collective, hundreds of souls racing together in one consciousness. She spread her arms wide, closed her eyes and leaned her head back into the wind that was rushing past. They were of one mind as they rode, connected and intertwined in the potential of what they were about to do. Even Liam's thoughts were aligned with theirs. She had never felt so free, so happy in her life.

The sky behind them was just beginning to reveal the first signs of day when they reached the Paris city limits. But the sky was still more black than anything. It didn't matter.

All Joel's senses were heightened, so he heard it before anyone else, the faint piercing noise in the distance. The demons had been tracking them for over an hour now but they'd only just begun to call to catch up. From the rear view mirror, Joel could just make out the faintest, growing dot in between the dark clouds.

"Let them come," he thought, with his eyes burning like flames.

CHAPTER 21: STRANGE FIRE

At three in the morning, Andreas finally found what he was looking for.

"I've located them," he announced proudly. Saubos stood behind him with an unreadable expression.

"Show me. Where are they?" Saubos replied as he scanned the satellite imagery display from over Andreas' shoulder.

"There," Andreas pointed. "You see those little bright dots? That's them."

When Saubos didn't respond, Andreas decided that he wasn't going to let Saubos' pensiveness dampen his elation.

"After all this time, they're finally going to come to us."

"Yes," Saubos admitted. "You have been very useful. Though some doubted, you have lived up to Crane's regard for you."

"I was thinking we could take them out with some tranquilizers or maybe some Luridium to neutralize them, clean and simple. A camera crew should be there to capture the entire ordeal. I'll make a brief statement, of course, assuring the public-"

"That won't be necessary," Saubos interrupted.

"Oh, I think so. Their surrender is becoming very unpopular with the public. After the killing spree your…kind went on after the attacks on the Quarantine stations, we can't afford to have some kid with a camera shape the story. If we're going to regain control of the situation, we need to rebuild our image."

Saubos attempted his best version of a smile.

"Another useful suggestion, but I believe our arrangement has come to an end."

Andreas didn't fully understand what he was saying until Saubos stepped towards him.

"Wait! What? I did everything you asked!"

"Yes, after many missteps, the last of which was almost killing Deidra Pile before she could tell us how she tampered with the Luridium samples. That would have been useful information to have." Saubos replied calmly.

"But I handled it," Andreas scrambled. "I caught it, didn't I? I switched the doses back. I don't know how she survived the Luridium dose I gave her, but the doctors say they don't think she will last the next couple of days."

"It is irrelevant. We will silence her permanently after we retrieve the Seers. But first, we are taking over the management of the Guild and the Seers. We've already replaced most of your staff who handled day-to-day management. Once we have the Lost Seers, nothing like this will ever happen again."

"Management of the Seers is one thing, but how do you plan to take over the Guild? No one knows you! They'll never trust you. I'm the one they trust!" Andreas spat.

"Yes, you are," Saubos said as he morphed into an indistinguishable image of Andreas right before his eyes. The last thing Andreas saw was his own image reaching out to snap his neck.

●●···●●

Since Andreas found out and alerted Saubos to the potential that Deidra had tampered with the Luridium supply, the Guild's Seers were more heavily guarded than ever before, with most of the guards being replaced by demons who took on the appearance of their predecessors.

Patience, planning, and destiny had set everything exactly where it was supposed to be.

The treatment from the Restoration Project, combined with the mutation in Lilli's blood, created a serum that neutralized the Luridium in the Guild's Seers' bloodstream, allowing them to access the Collective and the full extent of their power without the need for withdrawal. Once they received the serum in their bodies, the resistance to the Luridium became permanent, even if the original dosage was later reintroduced.

Now all Joel and the others needed to do was show them the way.

One-by-one, Joel, Lilli, Michael, Nina, Maura, Tenzen, and Katia closed their eyes, giving into the heightened consciousness that only transcendence could bring. Their minds stretched out as one, past the limits of what their bodies could contain, and seized those who were now ready to join them.

●●··●●

"Something's wrong. We can't get a reading on them," Patrick mumbled, more to himself than Saubos. His head turned between his control board and the Visioning Room in confusion.

"What do you mean?" Saubos asked. "Is your equipment working properly?" He still wasn't used to the sound of Andreas' voice coming out of his mouth.

"It is, sir. I've recalibrated about five times now and nothing. It's as if they're not there. The system can't read them, like the Luridium isn't present in their bodies."

Saubos' jaw locked in anger as he turned from Patrick to the visioning room. His eyes cast over the group of seven, scrutinizing their faces for any explanation of what was happening. And then they did something they'd never done before in Quorum.

Saubos watched in horror as the Seers closed their eyes in unison and slowly came together to join hands. Their heads fell back and their mouths parted in expressions of ecstasy and revelation, then their bodies began to glow within the dim light of the room.

"Get the tranquilizers! Now! Now!" Saubos yelled. "And call the others!"

"Who?" Patrick asked, watching the scene taking place in the visioning room with fascination.

"Everyone!" Saubos roared, slapping Patrick across the face with such force he fell backwards into his desk. "Every Purification Center! We've been compromised!"

Saubos turned and ran to the supply closet, hoping it was not too late. He grabbed a pack of tranquilizers and a gun and returned in time to hear Patrick trying to decipher the babbling of someone on the other end of the speakerphone.

"What's happening? We can't get a reading on them. We can't. Oh my God! Oh my God! They're changing. They're..."

Saubos didn't wait to hear anymore as he pushed past Patrick and opened the door to the visioning room.

In Prime there was no sound, only understanding and knowledge passed effortlessly from mind to mind. But as the Collective expanded with the addition of each of the Guild's Quorums, Joel could almost hear a rhythm emerge within their thoughts, like the sound of slow running water, gently washing away their distinctions so that they were one mind, one body, with one purpose.

Within the Purification Centers, those who were not in Quorum began to see the demons clearly standing guard outside their private doors, masquerading as men. Understanding what needed to be done, they drew closer, opening their doors so that they could be heard.

The words… we must say the words so that they can hear.

"Come to me. Show yourself." The whisper reverberated throughout the Collective until they spoke as one to those who were unable to resist the power of their voice.

"Come to me. Show yourself. Come to me," they chanted.

And helplessly, the demons were drawn, with the agony of their transformation on display for everyone who was close enough to witness it.

"Come to me," they chanted until each of them was near.

In Paris, the dawn was black with the thrashing of wings. The demons circled and hissed in useless resistance around the band of seven Seers who stood below them, infinitesimal in size, yet infinite in power.

All across the world, the Seers' hands reached up in unison, drawing the demons closer. The feeling was unbound, as if each of them was a part of everything, from the delicate ice crystal in the sky to the rotation of the earth beneath their feet and the awareness of everything that had been and would be.

The barrier of their skin was barely visible within the brilliant light that they had begun to generate. All they had to do was let go of the last thread of their humanity, the part that was afraid to die.

"Do not be afraid," they heard a voice speak into the Collective. "I stand with you now, as the last Seer, to bring you home."

The presence was powerful and reassuring—familiar to Joel and Lilli in a way that only one soul could be—Marcus.

"Come with me and show this world what they can be," his voice beckoned.

Lilli opened her eyes to take one final look towards where her brother stood. He was on the roof of one of the last remaining buildings looking down on her with awe and wonder that shone in his tears. Though he was far away, she had no trouble seeing him. Her presence had already expanded beyond the distance between them.

He was holding Alessandra tightly in front of him as she covered them both with a shield that trembled with her own intense emotion.

I love you always, Liam. Always. She whispered into his mind. Liam didn't have the strength to answer right away when he heard her voice. But as he wrapped his arms tighter around his wife and child, he finally understood.

Smiling, he let his thoughts speak for him.

Go, Lilli. Be everything now. Go.

For a moment, everything went still. The birds didn't sing and the animals didn't move and the demons were finally silent as the light of the Seers swelled to cleanse the earth of the evil in their path.

And when the dust from the explosions settled, for the world that had witnessed the sacrifice the Seers made to save them, it was a new day.

Epilogue: Order of the Seers

No one would've thought that it was possible to change the world in one day, but that was exactly what happened.

The first footage of the Seers' deaths surfaced less than 15 minutes after they were gone, with more videos posting with every hour that passed. The images they projected were stark, unbelievable, but also undeniable. The reality that a people so enslaved and mistreated would willingly sacrifice themselves for a world that denied them was profound, resonating deeply within the consciousness of the world.

Calls for the dissolution of the UWO and the Guild were as fierce as the cries to hear from survivors, those who knew the Seers who had died and understood the potential of the Restoration Project. Eli, Ngozi, Alessandra, Hasaam, and Neva, along with all those who had successfully completed the Restoration treatment, finally came out of hiding to show the world more possibilities for mankind than they had ever fathomed before.

The surrender of those in power to an interim government took almost a year to achieve. Some authorities, like Deidra Pile who survived Andreas' attack, sought out peaceful transitions, while other disputes could only be settled with violence. But the determination to find another way was unstoppable. The death of the Seers had issued a call that would not rest until it was answered.

A year after their deaths, the Order of the Seers was formed to help create a new foundation of governance. The Order was made up of those who volunteered to lead and serve through completing the Restoration process. Though Marshall and the first volunteers for the Restoration Project never developed the breadth of powers that those who were born with the ability could achieve, they were no less capable of extraordinary visioning ability. And as they achieved full command of their sight, they were able to show the way for many who chose to undertake the process.

Marcesa Lillith Knight was born into a new era of hope, and while life was far from settled, the new course upon which the world was embarking was set.

The fact that she arrived almost two months early was not a surprise. Eli had been tracking Alessandra's pregnancy since the day Liam and Alessandra returned from Nepal. In every check-up, his findings were always the same, Marcesa's physical development was advanced, more advanced than any case he'd ever seen.

By the time she was born with one brown eye and one green eye, there was little doubt that she was a Seer. And while her physical growth stabilized after her birth, her mental development accelerated. At just a few weeks old, she was already performing tasks that were not expected in a six-month-old.

When the Guild's files were seized by the interim government, it was discovered that the Guild had not recorded a baby born with the genetic marker in over three months. This in itself was not unusual given the rare occurrence of Seers among the general population, but it did cause concern when the gap increased to over nine months until it was finally accepted that there would be no more Seers born with the gift. Those who wished would have to look to the Restoration Project to develop the talents that lay dormant inside them.

Both Alessandra and Liam agreed to keep Marcesa's extraordinary ability, as well as the fact that she was the last-born Seer, a secret that would be hers to reveal if and when she chose to.

Alessandra served as the head of the Order of the Seers for many years, helping others find their potential and use it to build a better world. Liam found his calling in helping to rebuild the many cities and towns that had been destroyed by the demons.

Alessandra often travelled to different locations to help establish new branches of the Order that would help to set up and oversee government structures. But wherever she went, they all went. They travelled, worked, studied, and played together.

Often when Marcesa was finished with school, Liam would take her on long walks and tell her stories about his childhood, his family, and all the people she would never know, who were as much a part of her as he was.

But despite the peace around them, sometimes he still woke up in fear, drenched with sweat while remembering the sight of demons hovering over Lilli, Joel, and the others. In his nightmare the demons devoured them, while he screamed, unable to do anything about it.

On those nights, he would walk to Marcesa's room and watch her sleeping peacefully in her bed. He knew all their hopes and dreams lived inside her still, and it gave him courage to remember what he'd told Marcesa once when she asked him why they died.

He'd thought about the answer for a long time, wondering how to collapse all they had been through, all they had done into a truth she could understand.

"They died to give us something we couldn't see any other way," he finally said one night while putting her to bed.

"What couldn't we see, Papa?" she had asked.

"That each of us is infinite and capable of wonders."